The Amateur Executioner

Enoch Hale Meets Sherlock Holmes

Dan Andriacco and Kieran McMullen

Dan Andriacco and Kieran McMullen

Paperback ISBN 9781780924014
ePub ISBN 9781780924021
PDF ISBN 9781780924038

Published in the UK by MX Publishing
335 Princess Park Manor, Royal Drive,
London, N11 3GX
www.mxpublishing.co.uk
Cover design by www.staunch.com

Grateful acknowledgment to Conan Doyle Estate Ltd. for the use of the Sherlock Holmes characters created by Sir Arthur Conan Doyle.

Dan Andriacco dedicates this book to

CAROLYN AND JOEL SENTER

Kieran McMullen dedicates this book to

EILEEN C. McMULLEN

Dan Andriacco and Kieran McMullen

CONTENTS

5

Dan Andriacco and Kieran McMullen

Dan Andriacco and Kieran McMullen

ONE
No Escape from Death

"The Press, Watson, is a most valuable institution, if
only you know how to use it."
  – Sherlock Holmes, "The Adventure of the
  Six Napoleons"

Enoch Hale had seen death before, not long ago in
the Great War, but this was different.

The body of the man who had been William Powers
swayed above him, hanging from a noose. The face was
blue, the eyes bulging. A kicked-over chair lay beneath the
dangling corpse.

The American journalist was lighting a panatela to
steady his nerves when he heard a voice behind him. "He
was supposed to be an escape artist. I guess there's no
escape from death."

Hale looked around. Chief Inspector Henry
Wiggins, a wiry, middle-aged man with sandy hair, was a

hard-boiled egg for sure. The word among Hale's reporter friends on Fleet Street was that he'd once been a street Arab, practically raised himself from a young age.

"What brings the Yard's brightest out on a suicide, Wiggins?"

Wiggins was known as a master organizer, who might have risen even higher at the Yard if not for his independent streak.

"Just my luck. I was here for the second show."

Well, well, Hale mused, *it seems that even Wiggins needs a little entertainment now and then.* The Alhambra Variety Hall had been offering Londoners an unending stream of singers, jugglers, magicians, acrobats, dancers, comedians, and the like since 1854. In its time the hall had introduced Jules Leotard, the "daring young man on the flying trapeze," and the risqué "can-can" dancers (which cost the Alhambra its dancing license in 1870). The Moorish-style building, named for a palace in Granada, brought a touch of the exotic to Leicester Square with its two towers and a huge dome.

When Hale had heard from one of Wiggins's subordinates that a dead body had been found at the Alhambra, he'd had visions of a major scoop. The reality, suicide of a minor performer, was hardly a story at all. Still, he was here now, and who could tell what he might be able to make of it.

"So he hanged himself between performances?" Hale asked.

They were standing in the dead man's dressing room, a small chamber with almost no personal touches save for a theatrical poster rather hollowly boasting of "The Power of Powers, the British Houdini."

Wiggins sighed. "Doesn't sound quite right, does it? Suicides do strange things, though. Maybe the size of the audience at the first show pushed him over the edge. The real Houdini is pulling them in over at the Hippodrome, you know."

The chief inspector explained that twenty years ago, in 1900, the brash American Harry Houdini had appeared here at the Alhambra. The hall's manager at the time, C. Dundas Slater, had arranged with Superintendent William Melville for Houdini to be put in handcuffs at Scotland Yard as a publicity stunt. The escape artist had the darbies off before Slater and Melville could leave the room. The newly crowned "Handcuff King" had wound up being booked at the Alhambra for six months. This time around, now world famous, he was performing his escapes at a competing hall.

Hale stuck the panatela in this mouth and pulled out a Moleskine notebook. "Who found the body?"

"Singer named Sadie Briggs."

"Can I talk to her?"

Wiggins regarded Hale with his best attempt to look stern. "Cheeky journalist! How did you get in here, anyway?"

"It's my natural charm, Wiggins."

Standing almost six feet and looking taller because of his ramrod straight posture, Hale had plenty of that. With his light brown hair combed straight back, blue eyes, pencil-thin mustache, and devil-may-care air, several women who knew him would have preferred his companionship to that of Douglas Fairbanks himself. But men liked him, too.

"You're a scoundrel, and no mistake," Wiggins said. "If you can find her, you can talk to her. She doesn't appear to know much. Our boys are finished with her. Just follow the sobbing."

Wiggins's parting shot was only a slight exaggeration. Hale found Sadie Briggs in an even smaller dressing room drying her eyes. He paused for a moment to appreciate the skimpy costume and the curves it barely concealed before knocking on the open door. With a start,

Sadie Briggs looked up with the widest green eyes Hale had ever seen. She was a pretty girl, several years younger than Hale's thirty, with short blond hair and fair skin. Her height, about five-six, was boosted considerably by high heels.

"Excuse me. Miss Briggs? It is Miss, isn't it?"

"Yes, but who—"

"Sorry to intrude at a time like this, ma'am. My name is Enoch Hale and I work for the Central Press Syndicate. May I speak to you for a minute?"

"You're an American!"

Hale smiled. "I hope you won't hold that against me."

"Oh, no, not at all! It's just that I don't meet many Americans."

"That's odd. Where I come from, they're all over the place."

"Where's that?"

"Boston." Somehow this conversation, enjoyable though it was to Hale, was getting way off the track. Hale tore his eyes away from Miss Briggs and looked at the nearly blank pages of his notebook. "I understand from Chief Inspector Wiggins that you're the one who found Mr. Powers's body."

"Oh, yes, that poor man!"

"That must have been awful for you. How did you happen to be in his dressing room?"

Miss Briggs looked offended. "I wasn't *in* his dressing room, sir. He was late for his curtain call. The manager, Mr. Pyle, asked me to look for him. His door was barely closed, so I nudged it open. That's when I saw—"

Noting that her tissue was a sodden mess, Hale handed her his handkerchief. She thanked him with her eyes as he she blew her nose.

"Why did the manager send you?" Hale asked. "You're a singer, aren't you?" How this might fit into a

12

story, if he wrote one, Hale had no idea. But asking questions was what he did for a living.

Sadie Briggs colored slightly. "Yes, and a very good one. My name isn't on the bill yet, but some day it will be. I wasn't to go on until later, so I didn't mind." She shuddered. "If only I'd known."

"Why do you think he killed himself?"

She shrugged. "I haven't the foggiest. I didn't know him very well. I don't think any of us did. He kind of kept to himself, not the sort of show-off you might expect for the kind of act he had."

"How old are you?"

"What an impertinent question, Mr. Hale! Why do you ask?"

Hale tried to look contrite. "Sorry. It's not my idea. We're supposed to put everybody's ages in our stories." This was true, but misleading. Hale would have asked the question anyway, although perhaps not so soon. Her feistiness made him interested in learning more about the attractive singer than was strictly necessary for journalistic purposes.

"A lady doesn't give out her age."

"Then I'll say twenty-five."

She gave him a murderous look. "Say twenty-three."

Hale didn't have the nerve to ask her whether that was actually her age. He really thought she was closer to twenty-one. He closed his notebook. "Just one more question. Will you have a late dinner with me? I'm meeting a friend in about an hour at Murray's Night Club on Beak Street. You'll like him. He's an American, too."

Miss Briggs regarded Hale. "But we've only just met. You're a cheeky one, aren't you?"

"Believe it or not, I was told that just recently. I'll file my story and be back for you in half an hour."

With a wave, he was out the door. Never as self-confident as he contrived to appear, Hale half-expected the young woman to call him back, but she didn't.

On his way out, he stopped and looked in at Powers's dressing room. Wiggins was still there with two other policemen. The body of William Powers lay stretched out on the floor.

"Anything new?" he asked in a perfunctory manner.

"You might say that," Wiggins allowed. He pointed at the prone body. "Item one: Powers was too short to stand on that chair. Item two: There's a bruise under his chin that tells me he was in a struggle just before he died. Item three: The rope fibers are going the wrong way for him to have done this to himself."

"What do you mean, the wrong way?"

Wiggin picked up the length of rope that was still attached to poor Powers.

"Look here." He pointed at the bend in the rope where the hemp had gone over the chandelier hook in the ceiling. "See the impression where the weight hung? Well, the fibers on the right are all facing toward the body. That means the body was hoisted. If it had fallen, they'd have pointed away."

"You mean you think he was murdered?"

"No, Hale, I mean I'm sure of it."

TWO
That Shakespeherian Rag

OOOO that Shakespeherian Rag
It's so elegant
So intelligent.
     – T.S. Eliot, "The Waste Land"

When Hale's cab pulled up later at the back entrance to the Alhambra on Charing Cross Road, Sadie Briggs was waiting. Hale admired the straight black velvet skirt riding just above her knee, and the shimmering top of gold silk. Over her shoulders she wore a black shawl of oriental design, seamed with gold and silver figures. A white feather was affixed to her hair by a silver clip.

"I was just about to leave," Sadie said pointedly.

"Sorry," Hale said, helping her into the cab. He noticed that her blouse had a cutout back. "I had to write a bigger story than I expected. I'll explain later. But I'd better prepare you for Tom Eliot first."

"He's an American, you said."

"Yeah, but he's such a cold fish that he seems English. No offence. My cousin Emily told me to look him

15

up. They were friends when he was at Harvard." In point of fact, Hale was almost certain they'd had an affair, but that's not something that was talked about in his proper Boston family. "Now he's unhappily married to an Englishwoman. He's really a banker in the Colonial and Foreign Department at Lloyd's, but he thinks he's a poet."

"You mean like, 'Ode to a Grecian Urn'?"

Hale was impressed. How many aspiring music hall singers knew Keats?

"Not exactly. His stuff is kind of untraditional." Eliot had given him a copy of a slim volume of poems published a few years ago. Hale couldn't make heads or tails out of it from the first poem. What kind of a name was J. Alfred Prufrock, for heaven's sake? Eliot had explained that there was a Prufrock's furniture store back in St. Louis, where Eliot had been born, but that didn't help much. And that third line, "Like a patient etherized upon a table"—that was the worst simile Hale had ever read, and he'd read a lot.

Eliot had said his mother was a poet as well. Fortunately, his father was a wealthy businessman.

"What about yourself?" Sadie asked. "How did you become a reporter?"

"By not wanting to work on Wall Street. That's the family business, you see. I dutifully put in a few boring years to please my father, but after a while I just couldn't stand it with the war going on. I volunteered to be an ambulance driver for the Red Cross in Italy. It was a lot more exciting than stocks and bonds, and it was. I wasn't the only American. One of the other drivers was a young kid from Illinois. He's been a reporter for the Kansas City *Star*. That sounded to me like an interesting job. So, two years later, here I am in London working for the Central Press Syndicate, firmly established as the black sheep of my family. How about you?"

16

"Oh, I like to sing. Journalists must meet such interesting people. Who's the most interesting person you've met?"

"You."

Her laugh was musical. "That was a good line, but you should work on the delivery. It came out a little too quickly. You're supposed to make it sound like you've never said that before."

Hale unconsciously stroked his chin, as if he'd been slapped. "I'll try to remember that."

Murray's Night Club, founded nine years before by an Englishman and an American, was considered the hub of the English dancing world. From the outside front it looked like a bank. Inside, it seated four hundred in a ballroom with a high ceiling, fancy chandeliers, a stage, and a dance floor. Everything was high quality, from the food and drink to "Murray's Frolics," a cabaret show with dancers and a chorus line.

Hale and Sadie arrived to find Tom Eliot at a table, wreathed in cigarette smoke and reading a book. He was a couple of years older than Hale, exactly the same height of five-eleven, and parted his hair almost in the middle. "You're late, Enoch. But no matter." He held up the volume so that Hale and Sadie could see the title, *The Mysterious Affair at Styles*. "It's a new mystery by a writer named Christie. I think she shows promise."

Hale shook his head. "You taught philosophy at Harvard and you write poetry. Don't you find detective stories a little low-brow?"

"Nonsense, Enoch. My particular interest in philosophy is F.H. Bradley's work on appearance and reality. Murder mysteries are all about appearance and reality. So are my poems. Who's this charming young lady?"

Eliot took a childish delight in reading detective stories. Hale couldn't wait to tell him how he'd spent the evening, but they had to get through the introductions first.

17

He pronounced the names. Eliot kissed Sadie's hand in a courtly manner, evoking a shy smile that Hale would have slain a dragon to earn.

As Hale stuck a panatela in his mouth, Eliot held up a blue packet of Gauloises in his tar-stained hands. "Cigarette?" he asked Sadie.

"No, thanks." She grabbed the cigar out of Hale's mouth and stuck it in her own.

Eliot lit it for her. "Where have you been keeping her, Enoch?"

"He hasn't been keeping me," Sadie said. She blew cigar smoke into the air as she crossed her legs, showing a gratifying expanse of thigh. "Nobody has."

"We just met tonight," Hale said. "She was involved in a spot of bother over the Alhambra. An escape artist named William Powers, the so-called 'British Houdini,' was murdered between performances."

"Murdered!" Sadie and Eliot said at once. Sadie choked on cigar smoke.

"That's what the chief inspector says. Sorry to spring that on you, Sadie, but I wanted to tell this only once. It's a hell of a story, and it's all mine so far. That's why I was late getting back to the Alhambra—this is a lot more than a two-paragraph suicide."

A waitress came and took their drink orders—a very dry martini with Booth's gin for Eliot, a Manhattan for Enoch, and a gin fizz for Sadie.

The band swung into Irving Berlin's "Mysterious Rag."

"That music," Eliot said, "it's so elegant, so intelligent, it should be called the Shakespeherian Rag." Hale wondered how many martinis he had consumed before they'd arrived.

"I can't believe it," Sadie said. "About Mr. Powers, I mean. Who would want to kill him?"

"You tell me, sugar," Hale said. "I didn't know the man."

"I didn't either, really. As I told you before, he didn't mingle with the rest of us much. And he's only been on the bill a couple of weeks."

"*Cherchez la femme*," Eliot said knowingly. "Wife? Girlfriend? Both?"

"I don't know anything about any girlfriend, but he was married. Brianna was his assistant in the act. She was on the sick today, though."

Hale wasn't sure what to make of that. Maybe if you were going to kill your husband and make it look like suicide you'd arrange a reason to not be in the vicinity of the crime. On the other hand, if you were supposed to be off sick, somebody might notice you all the more if you were in the building.

"Who filled in for Brianna tonight?" he asked.

"I did."

"You're a regular Jill-of-All-Trades," Eliot with approval, looking up from his martini.

Sadie waved the panatela modestly. "I'd never done it before, but there isn't much to it. I just had to smile, point at Mr. Powers at the right times, and help audience members onto the stage to inspect the knots."

This was getting them nowhere fast, so far as Hale could tell. At least the Manhattan was good. It amused him to think that back in Boston, or anywhere in the United States, he would be abetting a criminal act by drinking the cocktail. If the Volstead Act didn't get repealed, he might have to become a British subject.

"I suppose there are a lot of people running around backstage at a music hall, in the dressing room area and so forth," he mused. "There would be plenty of opportunity for one of them to duck into Powers's dressing room. What are some of the other acts?"

She rattled off half a dozen or more. "My favorite is Sophie Tucker, the American singer. She's wonderful. I don't much care for the male impersonator, Vesta Tilley. That song of hers, 'Algy, the Piccadilly Johnny with the Little Glass Eye,' is not my cup of tea."

"Do you think any of them might have done murder?" Eliot asked.

Sadie shrugged her shoulders. Hale thought they were very attractive shoulders. "I can't say I've thought about that."

"Scotland Yard will," Hale said.

THREE
Wiggins of the Yard

"In future they can report to you, Wiggins, and you to me."

        — Sherlock Holmes, *The Sign of Four*

Hale went to his office on Fleet Street the next morning with a spring in his step. On the way he had passed *The Daily Telegraph* newsboys hawking papers with his story on the front page under the headline **ULTIMATE ESCAPE**.

> William Powers, 55, known as "the British Houdini," was found hanged in his dressing room at the Alhambra Variety Hall between acts yesterday.
>
> "Despite attempts to make Mr. Powers's death appear to be suicide, there is no doubt whatsoever it was murder," said Chief Inspector Henry Wiggins of the Metropolitan Police Service.

The body was found by Alhambra singer
Sadie Briggs, 23 . . .

Less than half an hour after reporting for work,
Hale left for New Scotland Yard with Nigel Rathbone's
words ringing in his years: "Get the story, Hale!"

Rathbone, the frenetic new managing director of the
venerable Central Press Syndicate, was a Colonial recently
arrived from South Africa with new tricks for this old dog
of a news service. CPS had been around a long time. Horace
Harker was proof of that. The old man had been elderly
when Queen Victoria was still on the throne. He was no
longer employed by the Syndicate, but he still showed up
almost every day to stroll around the office in his shirt
sleeves and braces. He had nothing else to do and nowhere
else to go, CPS veterans said.

"Be sure of your facts, young man," Harker had
advised in a parting shot to Hale. With his potbelly, bald
head, beak nose, and wrinkled neck, Hale thought he
strongly resembled a turkey. The American wondered how
long before Rathbone's new broom swept the old fossil
clean out the door.

At New Scotland Yard, Chief Inspector Wiggins did
not seem either surprised or pleased to see Hale.

"You're late," he grunted. "I thought sure you'd be
here about an hour ago."

"The full English breakfast slowed me down."

"Saw your story. At least you spelled my name
right."

"Thanks. What's new on the case?"

"New!" Wiggins exploded. With his temper he
should have been a red-head, Hale thought, not a dirty
blonde. "Overnight, you mean?"

Hale eased himself into a chair in front of the chief
inspector. "I thought Scotland Yard never sleeps."

22

"That's Pinkerton, the private eye company." Even in England the wide-open orb symbolizing the American firm was well known.

"But you must have talked to the other employees of the Alhambra before they could leave. And how about the victim's wife?"

"I gave her the bad news myself." The expression on Wiggins's face indicated that it had not been a pleasant experience. "She's a pretty girl, much younger than Powers. She seemed genuinely shocked."

"But she performs on stage," Hale pointed out. "Maybe she was performing when she reacted to the news. You know the spouse is the most likely killer in any homicide, sometimes with a little help from a friend of the opposite sex." Hale had learned that early on from covering routine murders, of which there was no lack in London.

"Brianna Powers wasn't even at the Alhambra yesterday."

"Are you sure?" Hale countered. "I've been thinking about this since last night, Wiggins. Suppose she just pretended to be sick and then went to the Alhambra in some sort of disguise. A little theatrical makeup should be enough to fool somebody who wasn't looking closely."

"You have a devious mind, Hale. Still, it could be true. We'll make some inquiries along those lines. It's not like anybody was likely to be paying much attention in all that chaos of the dressing room area backstage. In fact, anybody with a good story could probably talk his way back there. The manager, Mr. Linwood Pyle, admitted as much."

Hale was giving his Moleskine notebook a workout as Wiggins talked. "Did he give you anything else to go on—backstage tension or romance or anything like that?"

Wiggins shook his head. "Powers hadn't been on the bill long enough yet to make anybody hate him or love him, as far as we can tell. And if he was stepping out on a lovely young lass like Mrs. Powers with one of the other acts, he was plumb crazy. But we'll keep working on it. Meanwhile"—the Chief Inspector looked across his desk at Hale with a curious smile on his face—"I do have a piece of information on Mr. William Powers that you might find interesting. It may have something to do with the murder, or then again it may not."

Wiggins stopped. Resisting the urge to throttle the man, Hale said mildly, "Okay, I'll bite. What information?"

"He was bent, crooked as a corkscrew."

Hale didn't know what he'd been expecting, but not that.

"You mean he had form?"

"That's the devil of it. He's done serious time. Inspector Jarvis, a very bright young fellow, has had his eye on this Powers for some time but could never prove anything. It seems that wherever he performs there are burglaries in the area, but the burglar gets away clean. Powers did a few days in jail on suspicion once, but they had to let him go for lack of evidence. Jarvis said that Houdini happened to be making one of his periodic escapes from our hospitality at the time, and that's probably what inspired Powers to call himself the British Houdini."

"So Powers not only got out of places he was supposed to be, but into places he wasn't supposed to be," Hale muttered. "The irony of that is actually rather amusing. But does it have anything to do with his murder?"

Wiggins sighed. "I wish I knew."

FOUR
The Smartest Woman in Europe

Madame Sosostris, famous clairvoyante,
Had a cold, nevertheless,
Is known to be the smartest woman in Europe,
With a wicked pack of cards.
        – T.S. Eliot, "The Waste Land"

William Powers had died on Saturday, August 7. Over the week that followed, Hale nagged Wiggins mercilessly for updates. Only by great energy and no small amount of creativity was the American journalist able to keep the story alive for two days before he ran out of excuses to write new stories.

All of the office employees of the Alhambra, as well as the entertainers, were questioned repeatedly not only about what they saw on the night of the murder, but about what they knew of Powers. A clear picture emerged of a man of modest talent and immodest regard for his own abilities. This was not unusual in his profession, however, and Powers seemed to evoke no great emotional response among his fellow entertainers.

Mrs. Powers, in the assessment of Wiggins's best men, was more shocked than grieved by her husband's death. She appeared to be adjusting well already to her widowed status. But if there was a new man waiting in the wings, he'd been smart enough not to show himself. The Yard was watching.

"Hard cheese, old man," Reggie Lestrange, Hale's desk mate at Central Press Syndicate, smirked one afternoon. "We can't all get the big stories." The aptly named Lestrange was a simpering fellow with plastered down orange hair and a round shape. "Egyptology, that's the new thing, you know. Mummies are all the rage now. Crime is old hat."

Hale resisted the impulse to hit him with a right cross. Old hat? What was new about mummies? They were nothing but several-thousand-year-old rags. But Hale knew that Reggie was proud of the stories he'd written about the smoldering rivalry between two peers, Lord Carnarvon and Lord Sedgewood, both of whom were backing major Egyptian digs with considerable chunks of their inherited fortunes. Apparently Carnarvon's pet Egyptologist, Howard Carter, was thought to have the edge on making a major find.

On Thursday, Hale's persistence in dropping by Wiggins's office through the week paid off when he caught the chief inspector on his way out the door.

"Can't stop now, Hale, but you'll want to come along."

"What is it, then?"

"Another hanging. This one on Air Street."

The very name of the street seemed full of promise to Hale. Just half a mile away from the Alhambra, west of Piccadilly Circus, it was well known for its abundance of psychic readers catering to the carriage trade. If there was anything hotter than Egypt right now among the wealthy and the titled, it was psychics and mediums.

"The victim was a clairvoyant called Madame Sosostris," Wiggins said as they climbed into his waiting vehicle.

Hale nodded. "Of course. What was her real name?"

"Mary Fogarty, a woman not unknown to Scotland Yard. Some years ago she was a spectacularly unsuccessful pickpocket. Apparently she found a new dodge."

Her home and psychic reading room was a first-floor flat in an old Victorian mansion that had been subdivided. It was right above Day's Tobacconist shop. A sign in the window announced readings by appointment. Several lower ranking Scotland Yard officers were already at the crime scene when Hale and Wiggins entered.

There were three high-ceilinged rooms in the flat—kitchen, parlor, and bedroom. The heavy drapes of the parlor were drawn shut, but enough light seeped through for Hale to make out a round table with Tarot cards spread out haphazardly next to a crystal ball. A zodiac chart hung on one wall, and Madame Sosostris hung from what used to be a chandelier hook. Despite the ravages of a strangulation death, Hale could tell that she was pleasingly plump and younger than he'd expected, probably under forty. He looked away.

"Hullo—what's this?" Wiggins pulled a Tarot card from the corpse's hand. It showed a skeleton in armor riding a white horse.

"That's the death card," Hale said.

"Well, then, I'd say that's one prediction she got right."

"The death card doesn't necessarily mean literal death. It can mean a major turning point in one's life. But whoever yielded to the dramatic impulse to put that card in her hand might not have known that."

"How do you know it?"

"Journalists know all sorts of things, Wiggins." Hale saw no need to tell the chief inspector that he had once been briefly infatuated with an amateur Tarot reader. The relationship had folded when Hale finally figured out that she was stacking the deck to produce readings pushing him toward the altar.

Hale looked about more closely now and noticed a framed lithograph on the wall opposite the zodiac chart.

"Horrible old hag to hang on a wall," he said pointing at the portrait.

Wiggins looked up from where he had been examining the hemp rope used to remove the fortune-teller from the land without spirits. He stared at the picture of the hag. She was old and disheveled, standing on a frozen mountain with a crooked staff in one hand.

"Oh, that's Cailleach. She's a minor Celtic deity. Controls winter or some such thing." He turned back to his inspection of the hemp strands.

So we both have a wealth of useless knowledge, thought Hale. He pulled out his notebook. "How long has she been dead?"

"That we can't say for sure yet," said a white-haired constable. "The body was found about three hours ago by a customer, Sir James Carboy." That was a cautious answer, and a strictly accurate one. Hale quickly diagnosed that the constable was intelligent enough to be an officer at his age. He probably had been too honest or too unambitious to move up the ranks. "Inspector Cloud and I took his statement and let him go. It was him, all right. I recognized him."

"Sir James!" Wiggins repeated. "Well, well. Our Miss Fogarty certainly has come up in the world if the Foreign Minister comes calling on her."

28

"Not anymore," Hale noted dryly. "And I bet he wasn't her only upper-crust client. That fortune-telling hokum is very popular among the gentry and the nobility, from what I hear. Powers was hardly in that class. I wonder what the connection was between him and this so-called Madame Sosostris?"

"Other than being hanged with the same kind of rope, you mean?" Wiggins asked with a heavy note of irony. "It's a little too early to say about that, Hale. We're just getting started here. Inspector Cloud is out talking to the neighbors."

"Then I suppose you don't know whether the tobacconist downstairs saw anything?"

"Can't find him," the constable said. "His shop was closed when we arrived. But he was here earlier."

Hale paused. Maybe it was time to take a step back. "Do you mind giving me this from the beginning, Constable—"

"Gale, sir. Jabez Gale. Chief Inspector?"

"Go ahead," Wiggins said. "I only got the short version from Cloud over the telephone myself."

So Gale told what he knew.

Sir James Carboy had testified that he arrived for a session with Madame Sosostris at one o'clock in the afternoon. He had been visiting her for several months now and had found her prognostications amazingly on target. Many of his friends were her clients as well.

Ascending to the first floor, he knocked on her door as usual. The door opened at his touch. He looked in, aghast at what he saw swaying from the ceiling. He ran downstairs, to the tobacco shop, and asked to use the telephone to call the Metropolitan Police. Sir James knew Mr. Day slightly, having bought the occasional tin of Bond Street tobacco there. Mr. Day seemed quite shaken, as perhaps anyone would be.

Hale had once seen Sir James close up at a public event. He smiled as he imagined the old boy in action. The crease in the Foreign Minister's pants and the ends of his white mustache were equally sharp. He'd been an M.P., off and on, since the days of Benjamin Disraeli. Hale would have said that he was nobody's fool, but everybody has a weakness. Maybe his was cards, and not in the usual way.

"Sir James went back to the flat to wait for us," Gale continued. "When we got here, Day's Tobacconist was shut up tight."

"Do you think that's suspicious, Wiggins?" Hale asked.

"Oh, I suspect everybody. What were you doing earlier today?"

That was as close to joking as Henry Wiggins ever got, Hale suspected. "I was in my office, listening to Horace Harker drone on about some big story that he missed years ago even though it was in his own house. Something to do with statues of Napoleon. I lost track."

"Harker! Is he still alive?"

That evening, Hale met up with Sadie and Eliot at Murray's. It was the third time he had seen the singer since the night of the murder. But he didn't feel like he knew her any better than the first time he'd laid eyes on her well-shaped form. She had a way of deflecting questions from herself, as if she was afraid to let him get too close. She always made him pick her up at the Alhambra so he didn't even know where she lived. From time to time he wondered if that was just a tactic to increase his interest. If so, it was working wonderfully.

Tonight she was wearing a pale gray fedora. The hat would have gone equally well with Eliot's double-breasted gray pinstriped suit, Hale thought, but it looked better on

Sadie. She reached into the pocket of his suit and helped herself to a panatela as soon as they sat down.

"How are things at the Alhambra?" Eliot asked as he lit her cigar. Hale hoped that Sadie didn't forget who brought her.

"Mr. Pyle replaced Mr. Powers with a one-legged dancer." She exhaled smoke rings. "Scotland Yard is in and out, but I don't think they've found out anything. In fact,"—she suddenly looked smug—"I may know more than they do."

Hale leaned forward. "All right, spill."

He was expecting her to say that Powers was a bit dodgy. He'd already heard that from Wiggins, but hadn't passed it on to Sadie.

"There's a rumor that he was involved with the IRA," she said.

"What, just because he was Irish?" Hale said. Some nervous Brits seemed to see the Irish Republican Army under every bed. The rebels had formed units all over England in the last year. Liverpool in particular was a hotbed of activity, carrying out arson, thefts of arms and explosives, and destruction of telegraph lines. But the IRA was active in London, Yorkshire, Birmingham, and Scotland as well.

Sadie looked sullen at Hale's skepticism. "I'm just telling you what I heard, Enoch. I don't say there was anything to it."

"You're a wonderful little spy." Hale took her left hand, the one without the cigar in it, and kissed it. "Have either of you ever heard of Madame Sosostris?"

Sadie didn't think so, but Eliot had a vague notion that she was quite the thing in certain circles.

"She was murdered today," Hale said, "and in exactly the same way as Powers."

While Sadie and Eliot smoked and drank, Hale told them how he had spent his afternoon with Wiggins.

"Obviously, the two murders are related," he said. "It's just not clear yet how."

"What are you going to do?" Sadie asked. She knew by now that Hale would be looking for a new angle on the story, not waiting for one to find him.

"I'm going to try to find out more about this phony clairvoyant."

"Tell you what," Eliot said, setting down his dry martini. "We should visit Langdale Pike. You never heard of him? Well, he's a legend, a fixture in London. For more than twenty years he's earned a four-figure annual income selling gossip to the more disreputable papers, gossip about just the sort of people who visited this Madame Sosostris. It's uncanny the way he finds out all the gossip without ever leaving his club on St. James's Street."

"Let's pay a visit to him tomorrow, then," Hale said. "Meanwhile, how about a dance, Sadie? I do a mean foxtrot."

"That should be quite entertaining," she replied, pushing back her chair and extending her hand.

"Why?"

"Because they're playing a tango."

FIVE
Weekend Visit

"At this period of my life the good Watson had passed almost beyond my ken. An occasional week-end visit was the most that I ever saw of him."
– Sherlock Holmes, "The Adventure of the Lion's Mane"

It was pleasant to Dr. John H. Watson to find himself once again within a walk of the sea, visiting his old friend Sherlock Holmes on the Sussex Downs. He set down his bags and looked around the villa with a feeling of bittersweet nostalgia as he saw the Persian slipper with the pipe tobacco inside, the violin, and the photograph of *the* woman. All these things Holmes had brought with him into retirement years ago. Baker Street seemed so far away now, and these remnants of those days only increased the feeling.

"You're looking fit, my boy!" Holmes said as he picked up the bags and took them into the guest room that Watson occupied all too infrequently. "The years have been kind to you."

"Nonsense," the doctor replied heartily. "I'm more thickset than ever and moving more slowly every day. You're the one who never ages."

And it was true. Except for the slight bend in his posture, perhaps from the rheumatism, and a bit of gray at his temples, Holmes didn't look anywhere near his sixty-seven years. Maybe it was heredity. Mycroft Holmes was seven years older than his brother and laboring yet for King and Country.

"I see that you have finally retired from your volunteer medical work at that home for convalescing soldiers from the Great War, that you have bought shares in the Henry Ford Motor Co., that you lost your most recent game of billiards with Thurston, and you have joined the Reform Club."

"How in the world—!"

Holmes chuckled. "Good old Watson! In a tired and cynical world, you are always fresh. Surely when a medical man begins a weekend visit with an old friend on a Friday and plans to extend it through Monday, and shows up without a medical bag or a stethoscope tucked in his hat, he cannot still be in harness."

"Well, that is certainly obvious, but what about the rest?"

"In your most recent letter to me you mentioned that you were thinking of investing in Ford shares. When I see you arriving at my humble abode driving a new Ford Motel T, it is hardly a great leap to assume that you resolved that consideration in the affirmative. About the billiards, I was even more certain. You have unfailingly played the game with Thurston on Thursdays for more than thirty years. Never once have you failed to tell me the outcome upon first sight unless you were not the victor."

"But how did you know about the Reform Club?"

34

Holmes sighed. "On that point, I'm afraid I must shatter all your illusions of my amazing abilities yet again. I happened to be in London yesterday, so I dropped around to see you at the Sports Club. I expected to find you engaged with Thurston, but the assistant secretary told me that you had resigned. For a small remuneration, he provided the additional fact that you had switched your allegiance to the Reform Club."

Watsons's countenance clouded at the memory. "They refused my nomination of Murray to be a member. I could never belong to a club that wouldn't have Murray as a member." Watson thought for a moment and a quizzical look came upon his face. "Since you didn't find me playing billiards at the Sports Club with Thurston, how did you know we still played?"

"Really, Watson. You do me no credit. You are a many of extraordinarily regular habits. The Reform Club has a billiard room, does it not?"

"Oh. I suppose that was rather elementary." Watson sat and took out his pipe. "But what took you to London? I thought you never visited the old town."

"I seldom do, that's true, but I had a meeting with my publisher. I am pleased to say that he wishes me to produce a revised edition of my *Practical Handbook of Bee Culture, With Some Observations on the Segregation of the Queen.*"

It was evening. Dinner awaited, a fine country meal of roast beef, roasted potatoes, boiled vegetables and Yorkshire pudding, prepared by Holmes's old housekeeper, Martha. And while the two friends ate, they talked.

"So, Watson, I haven't seen any of your rather sensationalized accounts of our cases in *The Strand* for some time," Holmes said lightly. "Does this mean that a weary public is to be rid of me at last?"

"Not quite. I've been engaged in other projects in addition to rounds at the veterans' hospital," Watson said truthfully. He also had tried writing fiction, without success.

35

"But I think I have a few more adventures to share with my readers—perhaps that business of Thor Bridge or the veiled lodger, with your permission."

"Well, we can talk about it," Holmes said evasively as he cut a piece of meat. "Now that I am no longer in active practice, I am less enthusiastic than ever about the attention."

"And yet," said Watson, with a note of satisfaction in his voice, "you have not completely lost your appetite for news of the bizarre and the criminal."

Holmes stopped cutting. "Why do you say that?"

Watson pointed with his fork at copy of *The Sussex Times* sitting on an empty chair. "Because you were reading your local newspaper before I arrived and it is turned to what is no doubt a 'rather sensationalized' account of the second murder by rope in London within the last week. I can see the headline from here, 'Death Was in the Cards.'"

Holmes clapped theatrically. "Watson, I have done you an injustice. You are not such a fixed point, after all. You have not only seen but observed, and from that observation make a sound deduction that happens to be accurate. Yes, it's true, I am quite interested in these London rope murders."

"No doubt you feel drawn to the murders because of the outré nature of the crimes and the unusual occupations of the victims," Watson said.

"Oh, I am very much interested indeed in the occupations of Mr. Powers and Madame Sosostris. You see, I have continued to watch the criminal classes from afar since my withdrawal to the country. Powers was a burglar of no small skill. Mary Fogarty, to use her true name, was blackmailing some of the most influential men in the country—or in some cases, their wives."

"A burglar and a blackmailer!" Watson set down his fork. "What a pretty pair they were!"

36

"Indeed. And yet, Scotland Yard seemed helpless to stop them. Both victims had their skirmishes with the law over the years, but the Metropolitan Police were never able to prove the extent of their crimes. I doubt they even know about the blackmailing ways of Madame Sosostris. I myself only learned of the noxious woman a week ago when I was approached by a lady bearing one of the most honored names in the country. Her desperation was such that I agreed to look into the matter despite my preference for the company of bees, but I had made little headway in helping my client. You and I have seen something of the like before, Watson—criminals beyond the reach of the law."

Watson's thoughts immediately went back to the late Charles August Milverton, to Baron Gruner, and to several others who had not been able to avoid justice administered another way. In each of those cases Holmes also had taken the law (and burglary tools) into his own hands, with Watson as his accomplice. Suddenly an idea hit him with the force of a body blow.

"Perhaps that is the meaning of the rope!" he exclaimed. "The killer has taken the law into his own hands as a sort of amateur executioner."

Holmes smiled. "Your way with words has not changed with the years, Watson. Romanticism has always tinged your titles, from *A Study in Scarlet* to 'His Last Bow,' not forgetting 'The Adventure of the Speckled Band.' Still, I must confess I rather like that phrase, 'the amateur executioner.' It displays a distinct touch."

SIX
Langdale Pike

London, that great cesspool into which the loungers
and idlers of the Empire are irresistibly drained.
— Dr. Watson, *A Study in Scarlet*

Unreal City.
— T.S. Eliot, "The Waste Land"

Arthur's, where Langdale Pike spent his days
collecting gossip, was a purely social club—not a political
one—at 69 St. James's Street. It had been established in
1811 as the first club formed by membership ownership.
After an initiation fee of £21, the yearly dues were £10, 10s.

St. James's Street was also home to the Conservative
Club and the New University Club. Just around the corner
in Pall Mall were the Athenaeum, the Reform Club, and the
Diogenes Club. This part of London was often called
Clubland.

So Tom Eliot informed Hale on their way to see
Pike the day after the murder of Madame Sosostris.

"And you say Pike has made Arthur's his headquarters for years?" Hale asked.

"When he dies," Eliot said, "I expect the staff to dust around him."

"How do you know so much about this gossip-monger?"

"Where do you think he gets some of his gossip? We bankers hear a lot, even in the musty old Colonial and Foreign Department. "

Hale couldn't make up his mind whether Eliot was joking or not.

Arthur's, a building fashioned out of gray stone on the ground level and concrete above, was four stories high but had only two floors. Four huge windows overlooked the street on the ground floor, with five more large windows on the first floor separated by six columns. In the ground-floor window closest to the front entrance sat Langdale Pike, watching London and collecting gossip for resale.

He rose to greet them, a diminutive man with a head out of proportion to his body and more hair in his gray mutton-chop whiskers than covered his pink scalp. His three-piece gray suit, the chain of a pocket watch stretched across the waistcoat, was of a style that suggested it had first been donned in the previous century.

The club was perhaps a century old, a grand old edifice of two-story ceilings, marble statues, imposing painting, and a grand staircase in the entrance hall.

Pike squinted, then smiled in recognition. "Eliot, my good man," he said in a soft voice, "what juicy bit of gossip brings you my way today?"

"The bit that you're going to tell us, Pike."

The little man's white eyebrows shot up. His eyes were cerulean blue, like the ocean. "You intrigue me."

"Have you ever heard of a woman who called herself Madame Sosostris—a clairvoyant or fortune-teller?"

"I imagine that everyone has by now." Pike closed his eyes as if to better read what was inscribed on his memory. *"The Daily Telegraph*, page one, lower right. *The Times*, page six, top left. *The Morning*—"

"Yeah," Hale interrupted. "The murder was well covered in the newspapers." He'd had the story to himself up to now, with the papers either picking up the CPS story or basically rewriting it without acknowledgement. But he couldn't expect to continue with competition for long. "What we really want to know is, had you heard of her before today?"

"Of course. She's all the rage right now amongst the smart set and the nobility. Many members of the Ghost Club went to see her to investigate whether she had true psychic powers."

"Ghost Club?" Hale repeated. "Are you serious?"

"Completely. The Ghost Club has been around since I was a boy. It was started in the early 1860s, I believe. Many learned men belong to the group. They believe in the spirit world and do very interesting work. They are as concerned about exposing frauds and charlatans as they are about proving the existence of another, umm, dimension, shall we say. Some prominent people are members, William Butler Yeats and Arthur Conan Doyle among them.

"Your friend Madame Sosostris was also a subject of that American fellow Houdini. It seems he is on a personal crusade to expose mediums and such."

"Skeptical inquiry is all well and good," Tom Eliot said, "but who was seeing this fortune-teller on a regular basis? Do you have any names?"

Hale pulled out his Moleskine notebook.

"Certainly." Pike held out his open hand. "But I don't work for free."

"Let's call it a trade," Eliot said. "I think the balance of payments is in my favor at the moment."

Pike shrugged. "You drive a hard bargain, my friend." He closed his eyes again. "Winston Churchill was said to be a frequent visitor, although I'm not entirely sure what kind of charms he was interested in, if you follow me."

"Who is he?" Hale asked.

"The War Secretary," Eliot supplied. "He's a bit of an up and comer. Used to be a journalist himself, and a military man, too."

"I can see where a glimpse of the future might be especially helpful for a politician."

"Madame's regular customers also included George Bernard Shaw, Sarah Bernhardt, and Edward Bridgewater, the Earl of Sedgewood. Those are the ones I've heard of. I could ask around, perhaps get you a few more names if you like."

"Please do," Hale mumbled, somewhat awestruck. Everybody in the civilized world, he was sure, had heard of Yeats, Doyle, Shaw, and Bernhardt. The name Sedgewood seemed vaguely familiar to Hale as well, but he couldn't place it. "Do all these sophisticated people really believe in crystal balls and Tarot cards?"

"Certainly not all of them," Pike said. "Some undoubtedly go out of curiosity or because it's a fad in their circles right now. But I suppose there are some true believers mixed in there. Doyle certainly is one."

"What do you think, Pike? Was she legit?"

"Legit? My, you are an American, aren't you, my boy." Pike reached into his cigarette case and was thoughtful a moment. "Well, I don't really know. I don't believe in it myself, but 'there are more things in heaven and earth, Horatio' and all that." Pike stopped to light the gasper. "Were I you, I would have a talk with someone in the business. A performer or mentalist, maybe even Houdini if you can get him."

But Hale had another idea—a certain music hall singer of his acquaintance.

41

"You know from reading the papers that Madame Sosostris was killed in exactly the same way as that escape artist, William Powers," he said. "Do you know of any connection between them?"

Pike shook his oversized head. "Just that I hear they were both a bit bent, not quite on the up-and-up. That's not much of a connection, is it?"

"I wonder," Hale said.

SEVEN
The Essence of Lying

The essence of lying is in deception, not in words.
– John Ruskin, *Lectures*, 1870

The woman who called herself Sadie Briggs felt a little flutter as she waited outside the Alhambra for Enoch Hale to pick her up for lunch. The flutter was in her stomach, but her heart was the real issue. It pounded like mad whenever she was near her American dream.

She'd never met a man quite like Hale before—handsome, intelligent, a good listener, strong-willed but not too forward with her, well-educated, and dryly humorous all in one package. He was also noble in the American sense, which had nothing to do with the British and European idea of "nobility" as something inherited for generations.

That's why she felt so badly about deceiving him. How long could this go on before she told the truth or he figured it out? She wanted to tell him but she hadn't the courage. He came from a wealthy background that he had turned his back on. How would he react if he knew what she really was?

She couldn't even let him see where she lived. That's why she always had him pick her up here at the Alhambra. Surely he must realize that there was something strange about that. He was a man who noticed things; that was clear from the details in the news stories he wrote. Those stories! It was a good thing Daddy didn't know who Sadie Briggs is! She would never hear the end of it.

But she didn't want to think about her father right now. She wanted to think about Enoch Hale. Even his name was wonderful, so strong and masculine.

And there he was! Tall and slim, he stepped out the cab with the grace of a dancer. But he was no dancer, never mind that he thought he was. Her feet hurt at the memory. She couldn't wait to tell him her good news.

"I hope you're ready to eat," he said, helping her into the cab.

"Actually, I'm not very hungry." That was just a small lie. She was almost four pounds overweight and determined to starve it out of her. It didn't really show to anyone but her. Styles this year were loose fitting with a line that went straight from the bust to the hip. But she knew she'd gained weight and that was enough. Those gowns she wore on stage would show the difference. "But what say we just walk to Lyons'? It's not far and we can listen to the music."

Lyons' "Popular Café" was a favorite middle-class café with seating for two thousand and a menu at reasonable prices. The café had opened in Piccadilly in 1904 and was more popular than ever. Its biggest draw was not only the food, which was good, and the reasonable prices, but the band which played for the entertainment of the clients both afternoon and evening. There was little chance that anybody who knew Sadie in her other life would see her there.

44

They walked the short distance to the restaurant in silence. Sadie, for some reason she couldn't fathom, wasn't sure what to say without giving away how she was feeling. When they arrived at Lyons' they were seated immediately. Instead of the regular full-size luncheon, Hale asked for the "pink card" for general food items.

"You look happy," Hale observed. "I'd like to think it's the pleasure of seeing your favorite American but it's only been"—he looked at his pocket watch—"about twelve hours since we parted."

In fact, being with Enoch Hale did make her deliriously happy, but she couldn't let him know that. She took a deep breath, and then blurted out: "Mr. Pyle wants me to sing, Enoch. By myself, I mean. A solo act right before the interval!"

"That's wonderful!" She felt a little tingle as he took her hands in his. "When do you start?"

"Next week already. That won't be easy. I'll be rehearsing every morning until then as well as singing backup at night."

"We should have champagne to celebrate." Hale craned has neck as if looking for a waiter.

"Oh, no! I couldn't. Not during the day. I'd get quite tipsy." And there's no telling what she might do then.

"I'll just get a class for myself then."

The flute of champagne and their lunch came quickly while Sadie bubbled over with the details of what she would sing, what she would wear. Their waiter, a Frenchman, delivered the food and drink with a maximum of fussing around the table.

"*Merci*," Sadie said.

"Oh, *vous parlez français*," Hale said to Sadie when the waiter had left.

"*Non, je viens de faire semblant.*" No, I just pretend.

45

The words were barely out of her mouth before Sadie regretted them. Music hall singers didn't speak French unless they were French.

Hale regarded her shrewdly, as if he were thinking the same thing. That worried her.

"What do you know about clairvoyants, fortune-tellers, whatever you call them?" he asked.

The question came as a complete surprise. "I think they're very clever frauds."

"You work in a music hall. Sometimes the halls have acts like that. Did you ever hear how they do it?"

Sadie chewed her salad thoughtfully as she listened to the music of the band and tried to remember. "One of the girls I sing with, Molly Davis, once worked for a clairvoyant named Professor Ben Sterling. She said he was really a kind of Sherlock Holmes. He would look at people in the audience for little clues. Once he told them things about themselves that they thought he couldn't know, they'd believe anything he said." This wasn't helping, she knew. Sadie tried to remember what else she'd heard. "He also told Molly that the other kind of clairvoyant, the kind that doesn't work on stage in front of an audience, can sometimes get people to tell them all kinds of information without them even knowing it, and then feed it back to them so they look brilliant. Does that make sense?"

"Actually, it does my poppet." Hale pushed aside his plate and lit up a panatela. "And it gives me an idea that maybe our Madame Sosostris knew more about somebody than she should have."

"And how does that fit into Mr. Powers's murder?"

"I have no clue. That's the biggest mystery of all." He smoked thoughtfully.

"Tell me about your morning at that stuffy old club that won't let the ladies in."

46

"Well, it's too bad they don't because you would have liked it. It's a lovely old building. That Langdale Pike is a bit of an odd duck, but he had the goods."

"What do you mean?"

Hale pulled out his notebook. "He gave us the names of several of her clients, starting with the Ghost Club. Yes, there really is such a thing, and some of the members visited Madame to check her out. Then there were her clients, including Winston Churchill, George Bernard Shaw, Sarah Bernhardt—"

"Sarah!"

Hale smiled. Of course, anyone in the entertainment world would be awed by the legendary Sarah, the most famous actress in the world.

"—and a Lord Sedgewood."

Sarah visibly paled.

"What are you going to do next?"

"I'm going to interview as many of those people as I can."

Sadie grabbed Hale's champagne and took a gulp. "I don't think you should do that, Enoch."

"Why not? It's how I earn my meager living, you know." His family allowance was far larger, but that was beside the point.

"But it could be really dangerous. One of those people might be the murderer."

Hale smiled, irritating Sadie. He was treating her like a child. "Surely not Sarah Bernhardt!"

"No, of course not her. But what about, well, Winston Churchill, for instance? My father says that man— Oh, never mind. What if he's the killer?"

"Then I'll have a devil of a story!"

"That won't do you any good if you're dead!"

Other patrons, who seemed to Sadie to include a large number of fat men and their mistresses, turned to look at them. But she didn't care.

47

"You should leave this to Scotland Yard, Enoch. Wiggins tells you everything they get, doesn't he? Why can't you just be satisfied with that?"

"For one thing, they're not getting very much. I saw Wiggins right after Eliot and I talked to Pike. The chief inspector looked pretty miserable. Apparently he's under a lot of pressure from the Commissioner himself, Stanley Hopkins. But he's only got one good lead. That tobacconist with the shop downstairs from Madame Sosostris has dropped off the face of the earth. His landlady said he never came home the day of the murder. Since he's not around to be interviewed, I'm going to talk to some people who are."

Sadie stood up. "I can't just stand by while you do that."

Hale rose, too, and stood very close to her. He was about a head taller, even with her heels on. She didn't mind that while they were dancing, but she didn't like the way he looked down at her now. "Then come along with me," he said.

"You infuriating man!"

Sadie grabbed his head, pulled his face down to hers, and gave him a hard kiss on the lips. He responded with enthusiasm, never mind that they had an audience. She felt herself melting. It took all the determination she could muster to pull away and give Hale an even harder slap in the face.

She picked up her purse and slung it over her shoulder. "Come see me when you've grown up, Mr. Hale."

As Sadie strode quickly away, she heard Hale laughing behind her. She could feel her face turning red. And she worried that she had overplayed her hand.

48

EIGHT
Politician and Peer

"Nothing matters very much and few things matter at all."
— Lord Arthur Balfour

An hour later, Hale was still smiling as he thought of Sadie's parting shot. What spunk! That girl was certainly a worthy opponent. And opponent she was. There was something fishy about her that he just couldn't put his finger on.

He knew almost nothing about her, including where she came from or how she'd spent the first twenty-some years of her life or where she went to school to read Keats and learn French. He didn't even know whether Sadie Briggs was her real name. A stage name wouldn't be unusual for a music hall singer. He thought about the initials S.B.

Maybe she was Sarah Bernhardt's love child . . . and her father was the late King Edward!

That was the kind of silliness that one was likely to venture into when one had no facts.

Well, what *did* he know about her? She was a good kisser and an equally good slapper; that had been established. She was also pretty, well-educated, independent, feisty and forward in some ways, shy and reserved in others.

Hale had known plenty of shy girls, and girls who didn't want him to know where they lived. There was more to her reticence than that. Every time he brought the conversation close to her, she skillfully moved it on to another topic. That wasn't so hard, considering that they'd met during a murder investigation.

So . . . did she know something about the murders that she wasn't saying? For example, was Sadie closer to Powers than she'd let on? If so, apparently none of the other Alhambra performers knew it. Hale didn't think that was likely. Backstage was probably an incubator of gossip, especially as concerned ambitious young singers and affairs of the heart. If there had been something going on between the singer and the escape artist, he likely would have heard about it.

Not that Hale was trying to play detective and find the murderer. What he wanted to find was a good story. That's why he had wanted to start by interviewing Sarah Bernhardt, the Divine Sarah. Who wouldn't? She was more than just an actress; she was a phenomenon. There was simply no one like her. Already in her seventies and with a wooden leg, she had visited the troops at the front during the Great War, carried through the trenches on a small chair. She'd injured one of her presumably shapely legs on stage in South Africa in 1905. It had never healed properly and had been amputated ten years later.

Hale had already known a lot about her—everyone did—and Langdale Pike had told him even more. The illegitimate child of a Jewish courtesan from Amsterdam and an unknown father, she lived in a convent as a young girl. At age sixteen, she had wanted to become a nun. (Pike got quite a chuckle out of that.) Instead, she became an actress at the urging of her mother's friend, a cousin of the French Emperor Napoleon III. A spectacular success on stage, she was making films as early as 1900. Her film *Le Duel d'Hamlet*, reprising her famous stage role of Hamlet, was accompanied by an Edison recording cylinder that made the actors appear to talk.

Sarah was rumored to have had an affair with Edward VII back in the 1880s, when he was the Prince of Wales.

As an avowed atheist, it didn't make sense that Sarah would have had any belief in Madame Sosostris and her supposed powers to predict the future. Perhaps she had gone there as a lark. But there was another possibility. She was a friend of Harry Houdini and his wife, Bess, according to Pike. Perhaps she had gone to Air Street to investigate the clairvoyant on behalf of the American escape artist. If so, that would establish a connection, paper thin but the only one that he'd found, between the death of the "British Houdini" and that of the second victim.

But that was a big "if." In truth, Hale had no idea why Sarah Bernhardt had visited Madame Sosostris and he wasn't going to find out. She was back in France just now, acting in a play. Hale would have to content himself with passing on his notion to Chief Inspector Wiggins.

That was a disappointment, but he did manage to set up interviews with Winston Churchill and Lord Sedgewood. Tom Eliot promised to try to get Shaw and Yeats to dine with them that night at Simpson's in the Strand. This would be a long day of note taking, but worth it.

51

Hale caught up with Winston Churchill, Minister of War and Air, in a small cloakroom in Parliament. The minister had warned Hale on the phone that he would only have a few minutes before he had to testify on the War of Independence being waged in Ireland.

"Pleasure, sir," Churchill rumbled when they met, his voice somewhat muffled by the cigar he stuck into his mouth in order to shake hands. "Always happy to meet a journalist. Used to be one myself."

The Minister was shorter than average height, clean-shaven, with a receding hairline. Always conscious of his own physical condition, Hale noticed that Churchill's face was filling out and he was a few pounds overweight.

"Oh, and meet Mr. Dabney," Churchill added. The lugubrious man at Churchill's side was a nondescript sort of average size except for his chin, which was large. Hale figured him for some sort of parliamentary clerk. But that was wrong. "Mr. Dabney is my bodyguard from Scotland Yard," Churchill explained. "He's like my shadow—goes with me everywhere, whether I like it or not, to foil the evil intentions of the Irish Republican Army with regard to my person. Right, Mr. Dabney?"

"Yes, sir." Hale thought that if the man ever cracked a smile it would probably break his face.

"Care for a cigar?" Churchill opened a handsome morocco case and presented it to Hale. "Romeo y Julieta."

Hale had a pocket full of panatelas, but he accepted the offer. "Cuban, aren't they?"

"Yes, I've been smoking them ever since I covered the guerilla war there in '95. You're an American. My dear mother is an American. How can I help you?"

"I'm not sure that you can, Mr. Churchill," Hale confessed, lighting the Romeo y Juliet. "I'm just scratching around trying to find a new angle on a story. I've been covering the murders of William Powers and Madame Sosostris."

"Oh, yes. Tragic, that. I've been reading about it in *The Times.*"

Artemis Howell, the *Times of London* reporter on both stories, hadn't done a lick of creative journalism. He'd been behind Hale a day or two all the way. But Hale swallowed his pride and went on. "My sources tell me that you were a client of Madame Sosostris. I was just wondering if you could tell me a little about her."

Churchill's beetled brows knit together like a couple of caterpillars mating. "Yes. Well." He smoked like a locomotive. "I don't really believe in that sort of thing, you know. I went along to keep a friend of mine company—Lord Balfour."

Hale had seen Lord Arthur Balfour in Parliament once, a distinguished man about Hale's height with gray hair and a mustache. Most recently Foreign Secretary until last year, he had been Prime Minister early in this century. Near the end of the last one, his term as Chief Secretary of Ireland had earned him the nickname of "Bloody Balfour" among his detractors in the Emerald Isle.

"Damn him."

Churchill's outburst brought Hale out of his revelry. "Sir?"

Churchill sighed—rather theatrically, Hale thought. "Arthur belongs to the Society of Psychical Research. He's been hooked on that hokum ever since typhus took the woman he loved."

Clearly, the Minister for War and Air would have an objective viewpoint on the murder victim. "What did you think of this Madame Sosostris?"

"I thought she would just as soon poison Lord Balfour as look at him," Churchill said. "It was in her eyes. I've seen that look before."

"In war?"

"In Parliament."

If Lord Balfour had been hanged and the clairvoyant still alive, Hale thought, that would be a great lead on the peer's killer. Even as things stood it was a great quote. He wrote it down.

"Was she good at what she did?" he asked.

"Oh, marvelous! She was highly skilled, could have been on the top bill of any music hall in London. Whatever future you wanted or feared, she had it for you."

"What sort of a future did she foresee for Lord Balfour?"

"A short one." He spread his hands. "Well, Arthur is seventy-two."

"What did she predict for you, Mr. Churchill?"

"Oh, the usual claptrap designed to stroke my ego. She said I would be Prime Minister some day. What politician wouldn't want to hear that?" He looked at his pocket watch. "I'm afraid I really must go."

"Of course. You've been most generous with your time." Hale closed his notebook. That's when he always asked his best question. "Why do you think someone would want to kill Madame Sosostris?"

Churchill shrugged. "Maybe to change her future."

Perhaps Churchill had something there, Hale mused on his way out of the Parliament building. Maybe the fortune-teller wasn't killed for what she'd done or what she had, but to prevent her from doing something in the future. Like what? That's where Hale stalled out.

Well, Mr. Dabney should take that idea back to Scotland Yard. Undoubtedly he'd already reported everything he'd seen when visiting Madame Sosostris with Churchill and Lord Balfour.

Edward Bridgewater, the fifth Earl of Sedgewood, held landed estates as well as his well-known interests in

54

shipping and coal. He had agreed, during a brief telephone conversation, to meet Hale at his London flat at teatime. The townhouse was at Number 10 Carlton Terrace and Gardens. The Germans had only recently reclaimed their embassy residence right next door at Number 9. Having been the German Embassy before the war, it had been used by both the Americans and the Swiss during the German absence. The rest of the townhouses were equally endowed with notable residents of title.

"He's still furious about the Parliament Act of 1911, which limited the power of the House of Lords," Pike had warned.

Hale felt confident he could avoid that particular topic.

"I must advise you," Sedgewood began as they sat down, "that I am not particularly fond of the Press with their sensationalism and their damned editorials, and I never read the trash papers." They were in an oak-paneled library, sitting next to a black statue of a cat. Hale suspected that Lord Sedgewood didn't read much of anything, including books.

The peer was a short man with a bit of a paunch almost concealed by his perfectly tailored blue chalk-striped suit. His blond hair was prematurely thinning across a high forehead. He was only in his late forties, Hale guessed, much younger than Hale had expected. Something about his fair features seemed familiar, but the journalist couldn't place the source.

"In that case," Hale said, "I'm especially grateful that you agreed to see me, your Lordship."

Sedgewood sipped tea, never taking his green eyes off of Hale. Finally, he put down the cup. "I don't cut and run. When the cobra raises his head, I shoot."

Hale was taken aback by the metaphor. At least, he hoped it was a metaphor. "I don't quite understand, sir. As I explained over the phone, I'm covering the rope murders and you were one of the latest victim's clients. I'd just like to talk to you about her."

"And who does it help to print that Lord Sedgewood is part of a murder investigation? My enemies, that's who! The unions would love to see my name caught up in scandal. Who's behind this?" His voice got louder and harder as he spoke. "Is it the communists in my coal fields or the Liberals that support them? Or is it that jackal Carnarvon?"

Carnarvon! That's why Sedgewood's name had sounded familiar to Hale. This was Lord Carnarvon's rival to see who could dig up the most mummies, or the richest, or whatever they were dueling over. Reggie Lestrange had been writing about it for weeks. That statue between him and the Earl wasn't just a black cat—it was the Egyptian cat-goddess Bastet.

"Your name appeared on a list of Madame Sosostris's clients, that's all," Hale said mildly, forcing himself not to respond in kind to Sedgewood's sharpness. It wouldn't do to mention Pike and burn him as a future source. "I assure you that I'm acting on my own initiative. The Central Press Syndicate is a news service beholden to no political party or ideology. It doesn't take editorial positions. Nor does Lord Carnarvon have any influence over CPS, I assure you."

Hale's usual approach of warming up the subject first with easy questions seemed like a non-starter with Lord Sedgewood, so he cut ahead to something that might actually produce a useable answer. "Do you have any idea who would want to kill Madame Sosostris?"

Sedgewood stood, prompting Hale to immediately do the same. "I find your answers to *my* questions quite unconvincing, Mr. Hale. This interview is at an end."

"Why did you visit Madame Sosostris? Did you believe in her powers or were you just curious? Were you looking for guidance on some big decision? Or was the visit related to your Egyptian excavations? Did she seem afraid of anything the last time you saw her?"

Hale was rattling off questions in desperation, hoping that one of them would touch such a sore spot that it would cause a revealing outburst from Sedgewood. The strategy didn't work. At some point the peer must have pushed a hidden button, for the butler appeared. He was about six-five and looked more like a prize fighter than the hero of those highly amusing P.G. Wodehouse stories about a butler that Hale had been reading.

"Show Mr. Hale out, Harley."

"I was just going, thanks."

Lord Sedgewood, calmer now, went back to drinking his tea.

Hale was glad that he would never have to see that unpleasant man again.

NINE
Poet and Playwright

There will be time, there will be time
To prepare a face to meet the faces that you meet.
   – T.S. Eliot, "The Love Song of J. Alfred
   Prufrock"

On the way to Simpson's in the Strand, Hale mused on the late Madame Sosostris's reach. Her clientele included men who would never willingly be in the same room together. Doyle and Shaw, for example, had had quite a public set-to eight years before over the actions of the *Titanic's* captain as the doomed ship went down. Bitter letters were exchanged in the public Press as the novelist defended Captain Smith's reputation as a hero against the playwright's scathing criticism.

Later, though, Doyle joined with Shaw and Yeats in arguing to spare the life of fellow Irishman Sir Roger Casement, a former British diplomat arrested and charged with treason two days before the Easter Rising in 1916. Churchill and Balfour, neither a friend of the Irish, had pushed successfully for Casement to be hanged.

Well, Hale had talked to the politician and the peer, now he would see what Eliot's literary types had to say about the murdered clairvoyant.

Simpson's, opened in 1828, was one of the first restaurants Hale had been taken to upon arriving in London the year before. It was best known for waiters carving beef at the table and for having been the chess center of the city in the days when Howard Staunton and his confreres had played the game there a half-century or so earlier. Hale arrived to find his dinner mates sitting in a booth that the great chess master himself might have once occupied.

Tom Eliot had managed to round up George Bernard Shaw and William Butler Yeats. Hale hadn't met the other two, but he knew plenty about them from Eliot and from their public reputations. Was there really enough room in here, or in all the world, for those three egos?

"Hail, Hale, the gang's all here," Eliot said, peering up through a veil of cigarette smoke. He performed the introductions as he lit a new Gauloise off of an old one.

"Thank you for coming," Hale told the poet and the playwright.

"It's always a pleasure to consort with journalists and other members of the criminal classes," Shaw said, stroking his trademark frizzy white beard. He was the oldest man at the table, almost sixty-four, and a literary lion if there ever was one. He was hardly less famous than Sarah Bernhardt, and just as eccentric. Hale was somewhat surprised that he wasn't speaking in blank verse.

"As a member of the Ghost Club," Yeats said, "I'm as interested in Madame Sosostris as you are."

Yeats, like Shaw, was of medium height and light build. He was about fifty-five, with hair that was graying but thick. He affected a pince-nez. He'd grown up on Irish fairy tales, according to Eliot, and now believed in magic and mysticism. Shaw, on the other hand, believed in . . . Shaw. He also claimed to be the reincarnation of Shakespeare.

The waiter came as soon as Hale sat down, having already served drinks to the first three arrivals. Shaw made no attempt to hide his disgust that Hale and Eliot ordered beef and Yeats ordered salmon. "Obviously I am the only man here who is not a barbarian," he grumbled before making his vegetarian choice.

After the waiter had left, Hale got down to business.

"I've been trying to talk to people who met Madame Sosostris in her professional capacity to get a sense of what she was like," he said. "Her real name was plain Mary Fogarty, by the way. From what I've heard so far, it seems that if she didn't actually have psychic powers she was rather good at faking it."

Yeats nodded his head. "As a serious researcher into paranormal phenomenon, I detected no fraud."

Shaw snorted into his Jameson's.

"What happened when you went to see her?" Hale asked.

"I was impressed," Yeats said. "She read my future as if she knew all about me."

"Bullshit," Shaw said.

Yeats looked offended. "She told me I would win the Nobel Prize."

"She told me the same thing!"

Hale felt as if he were losing control to Shaw. He looked at Eliot with a silent appeal in his blue eyes.

"Er, did she talk about anybody else during your session?" Eliot asked. Good question! Maybe she mentioned someone whose name hadn't come up yet.

Yeats appeared to think about it. "It seems to me we talked about Pound quite a bit, but I don't remember if I brought up his name or she did."

"Pound?" Hale repeated. The name was only vaguely familiar. "Is he a poet, too?"

Yeats nodded. "Yes, Ezra Pound, American. He's a very good friend of mine. I've known him for about ten years."

Hale remembered now: Pound was a friend of Eliot as well, and had helped him get that inscrutable "Prufrock" poem published in some little poetry magazine. Hale thought it likely that Madame Sosostris had been pumping Yeats for information about this Pound, which she would then feed back to him if the poor bastard ever got dragged into her parlor for a fortune-telling session.

The food arrived. Shaw looked positively ill as the waiter removed an antique silver cover, displayed the beef, and cheerfully began cutting slices for Eliot and Hale. But Hale suspected that the reaction was, at least in part, an affectation. Shaw was a dramatist acutely aware of the drama of his own life.

"I take it you went to Madame Sosostris as a skeptic?" Hale said to the playwright.

"I'm skeptical about everything except myself. And some days I'm not too sure about me. I don't believe in any religion, including spiritualism or any belief system that includes the ability to read the future." He eyed the vegetables being set down on his plate with appreciation. "I do believe that human life is superior to flora and fauna, but not by that much. There's a life force directing evolution toward ultimate perfection, that's only logical. I just wish to hell it would hurry up."

Shaw seemed to enjoy hearing himself talk almost as much as Churchill did.

"Why did you call on Madame Sosostris?"

"It wasn't because I wanted to know the future. That would be rather boring, wouldn't it? Besides, it's impossible. No, I went out of curiosity because I'd heard that Doyle was one of her clients. That lunatic is making a bigger fool of himself all the time. There's a rumor about that he's been commissioned to write an article on fairies

61

for the Christmas number of *The Strand.* Fairies!" Shaw chuckled, his eyes twinkling viciously. He speared a stalk of broccoli with the enthusiasm of a harpooner on a whaling vessel.

Yeats looked affronted by his countryman's scornful reference to fairies, but said nothing.

Well, everyone knew that Doyle had a strong belief in the supernatural. He had even contended publicly that his good friend Houdini must be using supernatural powers to affect his amazing escape. Houdini begged to differ.

"What was your experience with Madame Sosostris?" Hale asked Shaw.

"Oh, excellent! I told her my name was James Joyce. She believed me. So much for her psychic powers."

"She was a clairvoyant, not a lie detector machine!" Yeats exploded. "How can you expect her to read your future when you were deliberately concealing your present from her?"

"I didn't conceal anything important," Shaw pushed back. "I just lied about my name. That was nothing. I tell bigger lies than that before breakfast every day. I tell lies for a living, damn it. If her Tarot cards can't tell my future without knowing my name, what good are they? Maybe they told Joyce's future. Maybe Joyce is going to win the Nobel Prize, not me." Shaw's tone was jeering.

"What else did she predict for you?"

"Oh, the usual vague stuff. There will be a major turning point in my life. Things like that."

"You shouldn't dismiss the power of the Tarot so lightly," Yeats said. "You didn't hear the truth because you're not a believer."

"You heard what you think is the truth because you *are* a believer," the older man retorted. "A so-called clairvoyant makes a lot of general statements and your mind fills in the blanks. You go home thinking she told you all kinds of things she never said. Houdini taught me that."

Houdini again!

"Do either of you have any idea why someone might have wanted to kill Madame Sosostris?" Hale asked, trying to salvage something useable out of this conversation.

"I can think of a reason." Yeats glared at Shaw, as if daring him to disagree. "Maybe she saw too much in someone's future and had to be eliminated."

TEN
Death of a Printer

I had not thought death had undone so many.
– T.S. Eliot, "The Waste Land"

Ezra Pound had had enough of England. After almost twelve years of mostly living in London, and having just published the book-length "Hugh Selwyn Mauberley," he had decided to move to Paris. He hoped to find a better creative climate in the City of Lights. He would miss Eliot and Yeats, both among the few great poets of the day and discerning critics of his work. But they would continue to visit across the Channel as well as correspond.

And so on this bright August day, at six o'clock in the evening, the tall, hunched-over poet with the cat-like face and reddish goatee hurried toward Alcock Litho Advertising & Printing. He hoped to get there before closing time to cancel an order for some calling cards with the address of 5 Holland Place Chambers, which would soon be outdated.

64

The print shop was on Rupert Street, in the Haymarket area. Pound saw it now just ahead of him, with a man standing at the door. Peering through his pince-nez, Pound couldn't tell whether the man was just arriving or just leaving. Either way, he had his hand on the door, which meant to Pound that the shop was still open.

The man, apparently a customer, was even taller than Pound, handsome, and trim. He looked like a military type. Pound could always tell that sort. He had been a cadet at Cheltenham Military Academy in his youth, although it hadn't stuck. His attempts to enlist in U.S. forces in the Great War had been rebuffed.

Seeing Pound coming toward him, the man paused. "After you," Pound called. The other customer smiled and opened the door, ignoring the **CLOSED** sign in its window. Both men looked around the rather messy shop. James Alcock, proprietor, was nowhere to be seen amid the lithograph, letterpress, and screen-printing equipment.

"He must be here somewhere," the other customer told Pound. "He wouldn't go away with the door unlocked."

The two strangers walked together around the room as if they were partners, Pound carrying an ebony stick.

"Alcock!" Pound yelled.

There was no answer.

"Let's try the back room," the poet suggested.

"Maybe we should come back tomorrow," the taller man said.

Ignoring him, Pound went through an open door into a storage room with huge rolls of paper. Dangling above them from the rafters was a body whose face, even distorted in death, Pound recognized.

"I found Alcock," he said quietly.

"The big question," said Wiggins, "is how Daniel Day fits into this."

"The tobacconist?" Hale asked.

"Right. He's still missing. And it turns out that Powers bought his tobacco at Day's shop. So Day was a connection between the first two murder victims, a third point you might say."

They were standing in the storage room, where someone had tried to make it look like Alcock had hanged himself by jumping off one of the giant rolls of paper. The two men who had found the body, Ezra Pound and Commander Ian Bond, were still in the front room. Wiggins had interviewed them together and separately, but wasn't ready to let them go quite yet.

It was late Monday. Hale hadn't seen Sadie since she'd stalked off on Friday, but he'd thought about her constantly. He had even waited hopefully for her outside the Alhambra at the usual spot on Sunday, but she'd never showed up.

"What do you know about Alcock?" he asked.

"Not as much as we'd like to know," Wiggins said. "We've had our eye on him for some time. There are rumblings that these printing presses have turned out false papers and counterfeit bills, but we've never been able to prove anything. I hear that Special Branch is interested in him, too."

Special Branch! That meant that Alcock was suspected of somehow threatening national security. Before Hale had a chance to press the point, he heard:

"Don't you think there's some kind of modern Jack the Ripper at work, Chief Inspector?"

With a feeling of dread, Hale turned around to see who had asked the question. As he had feared, *Times* reporter Artemis Howell stood behind him with his notebook at the ready. Howell stood about six-three, stout, with a thick mustache and a penchant for puffing on a gnarled wooden pipe. A peaked cap hid most of his salt-

and-pepper hair. He wasn't that ancient, somewhere just north of sixty, but he'd been a reporter since the age of fifteen. In some ways, Hale thought, Howell's way of looking at the world hadn't changed much since that long-ago Victorian time.

"What do you mean, Jack the Ripper?" Wiggins exploded. "There's no comparison at all!"

"But isn't this likely to be a series of random killings by a madman?" Howell said, undaunted. He had a habit of putting words into the mouths of people he was interviewing. "This shop is halfway between the Alhambra and Madame Sosostris's, and about a tenth of a mile north. Doesn't it look like he's just popping off people who are handy within a certain area?"

Hale had been thinking a lot about Yeats's notion that Madame Sosostris, née Mary Fogarty, had been killed because she knew too much about someone's future. That was an idea that had promise, it seemed to Hale, whether or not there was any clairvoyance involved. Madame Sosostris had collected a lot of information in pursuit of her profession. Maybe along the way she'd learned something dangerous to the wrong person.

The idea of a random killer had never occurred to Hale. But now that Artie Howell had suggested it, the idea didn't seem too far-fetched.

"Any such speculation would be premature," Wiggins intoned. It sounded like a well-practiced line.

"Well, just how many more bodies do you need before the speculation matures?" Howell asked. "Is there a specific number on that? This is the third in little more than a week, you know."

Hale had to give the older journalist points for style. "Very droll, Artie," he said as the chief inspector regarded Howell with stony silence. "You should be a comedian in a music hall. I hear the Alhambra needs an act."

That would have been a great exit line, but Hale didn't leave. He couldn't afford to miss the questions and answers flowing back and forth between Howell and Wiggins. That only went on for a few more minutes, though. Wiggins answered the *Times* man's questions ("Who found the body? Who was the first policeman on the scene?"), but he didn't volunteer anything.

After several minutes of that, the two reporters were eager to interview the men who had found the body. They waited outside the print shop for about half an hour, while Wiggins grilled the duo again. Like any reporter, Hale preferred his interviews to be exclusive, *mano a mano*. But a shared interview was better than no interview at all.

"So, you're on the story now?" Hale said to Howell as they waited. Up to now *The Times* had been carrying Hale's account of what a *Times* headline writer had dubbed "The Hangman Murders."

"Like a hound on a rabbit," Howell assured him.

Finally, Ezra Pound and Commander Bond left Alcock Litho Advertising & Printing at the same time. Hale guessed that Pound was the bearded one in the pince-nez who looked beaten down. He didn't have a military air. Bond, taller and probably closer to Hale's age of thirty, looked as fresh as if he'd just taken a shower.

Hale had his notebook out, as if to announce his profession. "Spare us a word, gentleman?"

"Certainly," Bond jumped in. Even in the one word Hale detected a Scottish accent. "The word is 'good-bye,' sir." With that he stepped briskly away.

Howell, who was as tenacious as he was old-fashioned, wasn't going to take that standing up. "Just a minute!" He went after the naval officer, shaking his reporter's notebook in the air as if it were a sword of justice. Hale, grateful for a chance to talk to Pound by himself, didn't move.

"I wish I'd left England yesterday," Pound said gloomily.

"We haven't met," Hale said, "but we have a mutual friend—Tom Eliot. He talks about you a lot. I'm Enoch Hale of the Central News Service."

"Oh, yes. The Yale man."

Would Hale never live down his past? That had been his first act of family rebellion—insisting on Yale instead of Harvard. "Tell me about finding the body, please. Give me all the details from the beginning."

"There's not that much to tell." But he told it, beginning with, "I came here to cancel a print order." Hale interrupted occasionally for some clarifying questions.

"Maybe Alcock was starting to close up when he got distracted by a noise," Hale said at the end. "The noise drew him to the storage room, where he was killed. That's possible. What do you know about him?"

"Know about him?" Pound repeated. "What do you know about your bootmaker? He's printed some of my poems as well as my cards. That's what I know about him. Oh, there is one other thing."

"Yes?"

"He's dead."

Hale ignored the sarcasm. "Then you wouldn't know that the police suspected him of turning his printing press to illegal activities?"

"Like what, dirty pictures?"

Poets, in Hale's experience, not only wrote the strangest things but also thought the strangest things.

"Apparently Scotland Yard had reason to believe that Mr. Alcock was a forger and counterfeiter."

"That's news to me," Pound said. "He did good work at a fair price. We talked about poetry a little, but we never touched politics, economics, or religion, things like that. We didn't get personal. I have no idea why he would hang himself."

69

Hale looked up from his notebook. "He didn't. He was murdered."

"Murdered!"

"Didn't you read about the others? This is the third hanging murder in a little more than a week, and the others weren't far from here. There were attempts to make them look like suicide, but there's no question they were murders."

"I try not to keep up with current events. It just upsets me."

"All of the victims seem to have been a little dodgy. The one before this was a clairvoyant who went by the name of Madame Sosostris. W.B. Yeats and Bernard Shaw were among her clients."

Pound shook his head. "A rational man would say that a fortune-teller who didn't foresee her own death wasn't much of clairvoyant. But I bet Yeats was unfazed."

"That's a fair description. His belief system didn't seem rattled."

"Have you talked to Eliot about this? He loves mystery stories."

Hale preferred to be the one asking the questions, but he hesitated only a moment before answering. "He's been quite involved. In fact, he arranged for me to meet Yeats and Shaw over dinner at Simpson's."

Pound chuckled. "The yin and yang of those two together must have been fascinating, but it obviously didn't get you anywhere. The Yard is flummoxed, eh? I guess it's too bad Sherlock Holmes is retired."

70

ELEVEN
M

"The Diogenes Club is the queerest club in London,
and Mycroft one of the queerest men."
— Sherlock Holmes, "The Greek Interpreter"

From Artemis Howell's front-page story in *The Times* the next morning, under the headline **HANGMAN CLAIMS THIRD VICTIM**, it was obvious that Howell's attempts to pry a comment of any kind out of Commander Ian Bond had proved fruitless. There were no quotes from him. The story was a workmanlike piece, mostly accurate although the prose was literally purple ("As the body of the dead printer swayed back and forth high above the murder room, the face purple . . .").

Hale was more interested in a letter to the editor at the back of the paper's first section beneath the arresting title, **"Amateur Executioner?"** It concerned the Hangman murders, although the timing was such that it had to have been written before latest in the series:

71

To the Editor:

I have followed with interest the details of the so-called "Hangman Murders." This somewhat sensationalist title may be more appropriate than the authorities have considered. Both of the victims were hanged in a way quite reminiscent of His Majesty's justice. According to the news accounts published in *The Times*, Scotland Yard believed the murdered individuals to be criminals that avoided arrest only because proof against them was lacking.

Could it be, one wonders, that someone frustrated with this inability of the proper authorities has taken the law into his own hands. In other words, is this killer an amateur executioner?

John H. Watson, M.D.

"Well, what do you think?" Hale asked, throwing the newspaper on Wiggins's desk with the letter to the editor circled.

Wiggins read the letter. "Well, Dr. Watson's no fool."

"You know him?"

The chief inspector chuckled. "Since I was a lad. I could tell you a good story or two sometime. In fact, I'm surprised he didn't bring this idea to me. Perhaps he found it easier to write. At any rate, the doctor's smarter than some think. Mr. Holmes always said so."

"He's *that* Dr. Watson?"

Hale had read the Sherlock Holmes stories as a boy, of course; everybody had. But even though Hale knew that Holmes was a real person, like America's Alan Pinkerton in the last century and William J. Burns in this one, he had viewed the world's first consulting detective as a remote and almost legendary figure. And to think that Wiggins had known him! What had Pound said? It was too bad that Holmes was retired. Hale was inclined to agree. But it seemed that the detective's old friend, his "Boswell," was still keeping his eye on crime news.

"So you think there might be something to Dr. Watson's idea that the killer is a self-appointed executioner wiping out criminals that the Yard can't touch?" Hale said.

"It's not impossible," Wiggins said carefully, "but the good doctor's theory seems rather thin to me. You would think if that was the game, our man—and it must be a man, of course—would go after bigger fish. Mary Fogarty was just a pickpocket, and apparently retired from the trade, not exactly a successor to Professor Moriarty."

Hale had to concede the point. "But now we have three victims, not just two, and the pattern still holds: Alcock was also a suspected criminal. And that's the only thing all three have in common."

"That's not quite true." The expression on Wiggins's face seemed rather self-satisfied to Hale. "We have established that Alcock handled the printing for the Alhambra and for Madame Sosostris. So we talked to the manager of the Alhambra, Mr. Linwood Pyle, and he tells us that they only started having their printing done at the Alcock shop recently—at the recommendation of Mr. William Powers."

"So Powers and Sosostris both knew Alcock!" Wiggins nodded. "Maybe they also knew each other." Whether that was true or not, Hale realized with satisfaction that Artemis Howell's theory of the killer as madman who picked his victims at random had just been blown out of the harbor like the battleship *Maine*.

Hale had his next story. He stood up. "Anything else new, Wiggins?"

"As a matter of fact, there is one thing. We found quite a few unusual items in the late Mr. Alcock's office—wire cutters, paraffin, petrol, and fuses."

It seemed like an odd combination to Hale. "What would he do with all that?"

"Make bombs, most likely."

Hale was still chewing that over outside the doors of New Scotland Yard when two beefy gentlemen in topcoats, each about five-feet-nine and strongly resembling a bulldog, approached him. They had their hands in their coat pockets.

"Your cab is here, sir," said the one on the right.

"I didn't order a cab."

The one on the left, whom Hale mentally dubbed Tweedledum, pulled his right hand out of his pocket far enough to show a gun. "I'm sure you just forgot."

Hale had done a little boxing in college, but was no Bulldog Drummond who could take out these two armed bruisers and saunter home whistling "The Girl I Left Behind Me."

"I guess I did at that," Hale said.

He got into the black cab, but he didn't think it was really a cab. Tweedledum sat next to him and Tweedledee rode shotgun in front. Maybe be actually had a shotgun, for all Hale knew.

"You might find this hard to believe," he said as the vehicle pulled away from the curb, "but I've also forgotten where I'm going."

"I'm sure you'll remember when we get there," Tweedledee said.

Further attempts at conversation proved fruitless. Fortunately, it was a short trip. They drove through St. James's Street, where Hale had been at Arthur's just the other day, and into Pall Mall. Hale realized with surprise that their destination was another private club. From the brief glimpse he had before they ushered him inside, it could have been a Greek temple. Inside it was all marble and wood and silence. He felt a sense of relief, because he was almost certain that shooting him would get his captors ejected from the club for making too much noise. He'd been half-afraid that he would die without ever kissing Sadie Briggs again, which would be a great pity.

Tweedledum and Tweedledee swept Hale up a central staircase into a book-lined room on what the British considered the first floor. Inside, lounging on a comfortable chair, was a corpulent, elderly man taking snuff. He seemed indolent until he caught sight of Hale. There was a sharp look in his watery gray eyes that warned Hale to be very careful indeed. Hale thought of the alligators he had seen once in Florida, lazy-looking and slow moving right up until they attacked.

"Welcome, Mr. Hale. I see you've been reading *The Times* this morning with your full English breakfast. I presume you were gratified that your story was more informative than Mr. Howell's."

Hale tried not to look startled. "Since you know my name, it seems only fair that I should know yours."

The stout man inclined his head a quarter of an inch. "It is understandable that you should think so. However, we live in an unfair world despite my best efforts over the last half-century. My colleagues and subordinates"—he gestured with his flipper of a hand at the two men standing next to Hale—"simply refer to me as M. They think I don't know it." The Tweedle brothers looked hard at the floor. "You may find the soubriquet convenient as well."

75

What would Bulldog Drummond say at a time like this? Hale looked around. "Nice digs you have here, Mr. M."

"Naturally you are curious to know where you find yourself. Knowing what I know of your journalistic skills, I'll let you have the pleasure of finding out for yourself after you leave here. Yes, you will leave here. Your situation is not that perilous. For the time being it is enough to know that you are in a private club where no member is permitted to pay the slightest attention to any other member except here in the Strangers Room."

"In other words," Hale said, "there's no point in screaming."

He wagged a finger at Hale. "Don't be dramatic. I brought you here because I am an old man. At this stage of my life it is my preference and my privilege to do my business here rather than at my office at Whitehall."

"Just what is your business, Mr. M?"

"Protecting the Empire, Mr. Hale, and you, sir, are a danger to that Empire."

Hale smiled. "I find that hard to believe. I'm just a journalist."

M leaned forward. "To be more precise, you are involved in matters that, if you continue to pursue them, will leave you liable for prosecution under the Official Secrets Act."

All of a sudden, it clicked. "This is about Alcock, isn't it? What was he printing—currency, phony passports, what?"

"It would not be to your advantage to keep asking questions like that of me or anyone else."

"So who was he working for, the Bolsheviks, the Irish, anarchists or just anyone who had a dime?"

M sighed. "You are free to draw your own conclusions, Mr. Hale. Just remember that should you share

76

them with the subscribers to Central News Syndicate, you may find yourself in jail."

"Alcock was just one victim of the Hangman," Hale said, undaunted. "How were the other victims connected to this official secret?"

"The murders are not my concern."

"Maybe they ought to be. Whatever danger Alcock posed to your precious Empire, Powers and Sosostris may have been part of it."

M drummed his fingers on the arm of the chair. "Perhaps you have a point. Commander Bond could make a few inquiries. Meanwhile, I adjure you once again to be careful. My associates will show you out."

As Tweedledum and Tweedledee moved closer to him, Hale spoke rapidly. "You're not much for answering questions, but try this one on for size: How did you know that I read *The Times* over breakfast?"

M allowed himself a bored smile. "Your shirt-cuffs tell the tale. I always look first at shirt cuffs because they are so informative. Yours are covered first of all with newspaper ink. What newspaper would you have been reading but the one containing your new rival's competing account of the latest Hangman murder?"

"And the breakfast?"

"Newspaper ink isn't the only stain on your cuffs. One seldom eats baked beans for breakfast without all the rest. It has been a pleasure meeting you, Mr. Hale. But for your sake, I hope it is a pleasure that shall not have to be repeated. Do we understand each other Mr. Hale?"

"Oh, we understand each other, Mr. M, and your two mugs don't need to show me the way out. I'll find it okay."

TWELVE
Official Secrets

Of all matters, none is more confidential than those
relating to secret operations.
  – Sun Tzu

"The club is called the Diogenes Club and a queerer outfit never existed," Hale told Rathbone about half an hour later. "This man M is either a major wheel in His Majesty's Secret Service or he wants me to think that he is. He didn't say that Bond is one of his agents, but he implied it. If that's so, he was probably on the job when he found the body. No wonder he wouldn't talk to the Press!"

"Damned good work, Hale!" Being threatened with prosecution under the Official Secrets Act seemed to stimulate the South African. "What do you know about Bond? Is he still in the Navy or on some special duty?"

"I phoned our friend Johnson over at the Port Admiralty. He likes trading tidbits for beer money. Seems Commander Bond made quite a record in the late war. He stayed on board a sinking destroyer until it could be taken

78

under tow, saving a number of wounded men who couldn't abandon ship."

Hale pulled out his notebook. "He's a Scot, left the fleet after the destroyer incident, and went into Naval Intelligence work. He was mentioned in dispatches three times at Gallipoli. Since the war he's been seconded to some kind of special intelligence unit. Johnson didn't know what they exactly do. He sees Bond now and again in uniform at the Admiralty with a portly fellow he doesn't know. I'm afraid that's all he had."

Hale slowly put the notebook away in his inside pocket. "I'm willing to bet the fat man with Bond at the Admiralty building was none other than the mysterious M."

Rathbone got up from his desk and looked out the window toward the bustling street below. "We need o find out just who this M is, or thinks he is, and how does he control a Commander in His Majesty's Navy. But don't wait for that. I want a story in fifteen minutes. Put everything in it that you just told me."

"I don't think that's wise, sir."

Rathbone looked at him with scorn in his piercing hazel eyes. "You're not going to crumple under to this kind of intimidation are you? I thought you were made of sterner stuff."

"I'm not afraid of anything this side of hell," Hale said with some heat, "but we're onto a big story in these Hangman murders and I don't want to get shut down in the middle of it."

Rathbone lit a curved pipe and drew in the smoke. "So you're recommending a strategic withdrawal?"

"You could call it that. I'll keep nosing around to see what I can find out, but let's hold back what we put on the wire until we get something that's really worth going to jail for. That way, at least the powers that be won't stop the real story."

"But you'll get beat out by Artie Howell in the meantime!"

Hale shook his head. "I don't think so. I'm betting that he was invited to visit the Diogenes Club, too. And I expect *The Times* to heed M's warning. Besides, I also have better sources than he does."

"So what angle are you going to pursue next?"

"I want to know why those three people were killed, and I think the way to get at that is to look at what links them together."

"You mean Alcock as the connecting point between the other two?" Hale earlier had filled Rathbone in on his conversation with Wiggins.

"There's that, but there's also more." Hale pulled out his notebook. "I wrote down several connections or possible connections, in no particular order." He showed it to Rathbone:

> *POWERS – SOSOSTRIS – ALCOCK*
> *Powers bought tobacco from the shop below Sosostris. Did Alcock?*
> *Powers and Sosostris knew Alcock because they were his customers. Did they also know each other?*
> *All three were shady.*
> *Sarah Bernhardt, one of Sosostris's clients, is a friend of the Houdini's. Houdini exposes fraudulent mediums. Powers called himself "the British Houdini." Maybe Houdini's posters are printed by Alcock.*
> *The Special Branch is interested in Alcock, and possibly His Majesty's Secret Service as well. At least two veteran government officials, Churchill and Balfour, visited Sosostris.*

"But that M fellow said they weren't interested in the other murders," Rathbone objected, noting the final item on the list.

"He could have been lying through his teeth. Hell, for all I know 'M' may not even be his real name. Maybe it's really 'Q' or some other letter. But I'd probably better not poke around that angle until I'm ready to go to jail."

Rathbone smiled as he read back over Hale's list. "The victims are also all Irish. But surely that doesn't mean much, unless you think somebody is out to wipe out the breed."

"All three?" said Hale.

"Well, their names are surely."

"Alcock?"

"Yes, that would mean son of Alan. Of course, Powers is a very common name in the west of Ireland. Lots of them were here during the war. They weren't drafted like the English and Scots. As for Mary Fogarty, well you can't walk around Tipperary without tripping over a Fogarty."

If there really is an Irish angle, Hale thought grimly, then "Bloody Balfour" and Winston Churchill already had a head start on wiping out the breed. The former had earned his nickname in Ireland. The latter had helped to create the infamous Black and Tans, a force of demobilized soldiers sent to Ireland to augment the Royal Irish Constabulary. The two of them should be at the top of any "kill the Irish" suspect list. But the whole idea was absurd!

"There may be some other points I've missed," Hale said. "I just wanted to put a few facts in black and white. It doesn't amount to much, does it?"

"It doesn't appear to," Rathbone agreed. "But you've got some questions there. Nibble away at them. Who knows what you might turn up?"

THIRTEEN
Leg Work

"Wisdom is not acquired save as a result of investigation."
– Sara Teasdale, *Gem Quotations*

As Hale thought about the mysterious figure known as M, he couldn't separate him from his environment—the Diogenes Club. Who would know about that? The answer was obvious.

He went directly from Fleet Street to St. James's Place. Langdale Pike, ensconced at his usual window seat at Arthur's, seemed pleased to see him again. And why not? Hale had paid him in cash.

"Ah, Mr. Hale!" the little man said by way of greeting. "I hope that your inquiries are going well."

"They've taken an interesting turn. Are you familiar with the Diogenes Club?"

"Of course. Would you like some tea? No? A pity. I find it so soothing. The Diogenes Club is our neighbor over in Pall Mall. I have had the privilege of being a guest in the Strangers Room."

"So have I, if you call it a privilege," Hale said dryly. "What do you know about a member there who goes by the moniker of M?"

Pike visibly paled beneath his mutton-chop whiskers and put down his teacup. "I don't know what you mean. I've never heard of such a person."

Hale leaned forward. "I find that hard to believe. You know everybody and everything in that world, or at least in our world."

Pike dabbed his face with a napkin. Perspiration was breaking out on his high forehead. "Apparently not. I assure you that there are some *secrets* in this world that even I am not privy to."

"I'll double your usual fee."

"Money is not the issue, Mr. Hale. It was a pleasure to see you again. I hope I can be more helpful the next time."

Hale had seldom seen a man more frightened. And yet, despite his fear, he had given Hale a clue—the slightly emphasized word "secrets." As the American left Arthur's, he became more and more convinced that this M was nothing less than the head of His Majesty's Secret Service.

Hale spent an exhausting afternoon pursing the two question marks on his list, starting with whether William Powers knew Madame Sosostris.

His first thought was to ask Sadie. But neither she nor anyone else at the music hall seemed to be close enough to Powers to know about any associates outside the Alhambra. Besides, Sadie would have mentioned it if she'd ever heard of Sosostris before the psychic's murder.

83

Still . . . it would be an excuse to talk to Sadie. But no, that would only set her off again when she realized that Hale was still pushing hard on the story. If he was going to try to get back into her good graces eventually, and he certainly planned to, that was no way to do it.

So he visited Powers's widow at their modest flat on Wardour Street in Soho, an area that was coming back from being among the worst in London for crime. Film companies and foreign restaurants, finding the rents inexpensive, were taking over the area.

Brianna Powers was an attractive woman in her early thirties, with auburn hair, a lovely face, and a figure that would serve as excellent misdirection for a stage magician or escape artist, at least to the males in the audience. Their resolve to keep a close eye on the performer would be hard to keep with a looker like Mrs. Powers on stage next to him. Or with Sadie replacing her, Hale added loyally to himself.

The widow proved to be deucedly hard to talk to about a possible relationship between her husband and the late clairvoyant of Air Street.

"What, another woman?" Her cry came out as half-sob, half-shriek, and fully Irish. "How can you say such a thing, you brute! My Willie was faithful to me."

They were sitting on opposite ends of a long loveseat. Mrs. Powers had her legs crossed, showing off a shapely pair of gams. She was wearing an appropriately black dress, but it stopped above the knee.

"I'm sure that he was never even tempted, Mrs. Powers," Hale said fervently. Good grief! When he'd asked whether Powers had known the woman, he hadn't meant in a Biblical sense. "I just thought that perhaps their professional paths might have crossed at some point. They both did business with a man named Alcock, so I wondered whether they knew each other."

Brianna Powers dabbed her eyes with a scrunched-up lace handkerchief. "I've heard of Alcock. A printer, was he? I thought so. He's printed Willie's playbills for years. But I never heard of Madame Whosits."

"What about Mary Fogarty?"

She crossed her legs the other way. Hale wished she would stop doing that. It was distracting. Could that be what she intended?

"I think I know about three Mary Fogartys," she said.

"This one used to be a pickpocket."

"That narrows it down a little, but not too much."

Hale tried not to seem surprised. Judging by the look of contempt on Brianna Powers's fair features, he didn't think he succeeded. "You needn't look so smug, Mr. Hale, with your fine clothing and your genteel airs. People do what they have to do to survive. Just pray that you never find that out for yourself."

The journalist took a breath. "Well, anyway, it's a common name. This particular Mary Fogarty and Madame Sosostris were one and the same. Does that help you any?"

She shook her head. "No. I'm sorry."

Hale knew a losing line of questions when he asked, "Do you have any idea why someone would want to kill your husband?"

Brianna Powers looked Hale in the eyes. Her own orbs were bright blue. "I haven't the foggiest idea."

"I think she was lying through her teeth, but I don't know how to prove it," Hale told Tom Eliot that night at Murray's Night Club. "I saw it in her eyes."

"About not knowing who killed her husband?"

Hale nodded. "She either knows or suspects. And I think she knows whatever link there was between Mary Fogarty alias Madame Sosostris and her husband. She overreacted to the question. So, at least I made a little progress with that line. But my attempt to find out if there was a link between Alcock and Day, the missing tobacconist downstairs from Madam Sosostris, was a total wash-out."

The long-legged gals in the chorus line at Murray's reminded Hale of Brianna Powers. He didn't think she would have trouble finding something to do in the music hall or nightclub line if she wanted.

"You mean Alcock's wife wouldn't give you an interview?" Eliot asked as he worked his way manfully through his third martini and his fourth pack of Gauloises.

"That would take a genuine medium, I'm afraid. There was a Mrs. Alcock, but she was killed in the Easter rising, one of about fifteen hundred civilians that got caught in the fighting. From what the neighbors tell me, Alcock didn't have a girlfriend and didn't smoke." Eliot's eyebrows shot up. "Don't worry, he did drink. But quietly. He kept to himself." Hale sipped his Manhattan. "So I've got a lot of facts about Alcock that don't amount to a hill of Boston Baked Beans. The same for Powers, as far as that goes."

The twinkle in Eliot's eye could have been caused by gin or mischief; Hale couldn't tell which. "It sounds like your encounter with Brianna Powers wasn't without its pleasures. Miss Briggs would be quite jealous if she knew you were interviewing such a comely subject."

Hale snorted. "Miss Briggs doesn't seem to give a hoot if I live or die. We had a tiff on Friday and I haven't seen her since."

"Have you tried groveling?"

"I will if I ever see her again. Say, listen, Tom, if you stop giving me advice about my girlfriend I won't start giving you advice about your wife."

Eliot took a swig of his martini. "Let me look at your notes again."

Hale handed him the little black Moleskine notebook in which he'd listed the connections and potential connections among the victims. Eliot studied it for a minute, then shoved it back to Hale with a look of self-satisfaction on his face. "Crime is the link."

"Of course crime is the link. They were all murdered!" In *vino* may be *veritas*, but gin and vermouth didn't seem to be helping Eliot at all.

"That's not what I meant. Powers was suspected of being a burglar. Alcock was thought to be a forger and counterfeiter, plus had what could be bomb-making equipment in the shop. Of course, all those items have other uses, too. Mary Fogarty, known to her clients as Madame Sosostris Diogenes Club—"

"—wasn't in that league," Hale interjected. "That's the weakness of the 'amateur executioner' theory."

"You have a point." Eliot studied his empty cocktail glass. "Fogarty was a former pickpocket and a clairvoyant who, so far as you can tell, never stepped over the line into illegal activity in her Sosostris persona. But if two of the murder victims were felons, it's not a big stretch to think that maybe all three were. Madame was certainly no saint, so maybe she was up to something on the other side of the law that Scotland Yard hadn't caught on to."

"Okay, then what?"

"Then maybe the killer is a crime lord, a new Moriarty, who's getting rid of his competition the old-fashioned way."

Hale reached over to Eliot's side of the table and picked up a book his friend had been reading before Hale arrived. *Seven Keys to Baldpate* by Earl Derr Biggers, the cover said. "Another mystery?"

Eliot nodded. "I'm embarrassed that I haven't read it earlier. Earl and I were roommates at Harvard. I did see the movie version with George M. Cohan a few years ago. What's your point?"

"My point is that I think maybe you read too many mysteries, Tom. If Madame S was really a bigger crook than

Scotland Yard knows, the vigilante theory is the one I'd take a closer look at. But how are we going to find out whether that's true?"

"I know a fellow who may know," Tom said. "He's a reformed crook himself. I met him through Pike. He went straight more than twenty years ago, but he still keeps his ear to the ground. If Sosostris was a major player, he would know it."

"What's his name and how do I find him?"

"He's called Shinwell Johnson, or Porky Shinwell to some of his old associates. I'll put the word out. Then he'll find you."

FOURTEEN
Blackmail!

With the glamour of his two convictions behind him,
he [Johnson] had the entrée of every nightclub, doss
house, and gambling den in the town, and his quick
observation and active brain made him an ideal agent
for gaining information.

      – "The Adventure of the Illustrious Client"

Two days later, on Thursday evening, Hale was
standing outside the back entrance to the Alhambra, where
he used to pick up Sadie. He'd almost given up on Shinwell
Johnson, having waited almost forty-eight hours for the
man to contact him.

He had thought he'd given up on Sadie as well, but
he found out that he couldn't do that. So he'd been in the
audience that night. She was still in the chorus, her solo act
not to begin until next week, but she sang like an angel.

An angel? Who am I kidding? Hale wondered. He
didn't know any angels.

89

"Enoch Hale?"

He turned around. "Who wants to know?"

"Shinwell Johnson." The speaker put out a huge, rough hand and Hale shook it. Johnson was a red-faced giant of a man who made Tweedledee and Tweedledum look like Girl Guides.

"Yeah, I'm Hale. If you don't mind my saying, Mr. Johnson, I'd been rather expecting you to contact me sooner."

"I had some checking to do first." Johnson didn't sound apologetic.

"Into Sosostris?"

"No, into you."

Hale liked this guy. "Since you're here, I guess I passed the background check."

"I have to be careful who I deal with. If my old mates knew that I was cozy with the other side of the law they wouldn't be happy about it. But that's not your concern. I have some information for you."

He named a price. Hale agreed to pay, knowing that the money would have to come out of his own family allowance and not the coffers of the stingy Central News Syndicate.

"Here it is, then," Johnson said. "Madame Sosostris, Mary Fogarty, was a blackmailer."

"A blackmailer!"

Johnson nodded. "Some of the richest and most powerful people in the country came to see her on Air Street. Seems she had a way of wheedling secrets out of them."

Put like that, it seemed so obvious. Hale had figured all along that the clairvoyant was good at finding out things. He just hadn't considered the use to which she would put the information. This news meant that any of her clients could have a reason to kill her, but especially the politicians

90

like Churchill and Balfour. It would be hard to think of any activities that would be considered scandalous for the poets and playwrights among her clientele. Well, there was Oscar Wilde . . .

But if somebody hanged Fogarty/Sosostris because she was blackmailing him, why kill Powers and Alcock? As a red herring to throw the police off the scent! That's just the sort of cold-blooded idea a man like Churchill or Balfour might come up with, Hale realized with growing excitement.

This could be big, even big enough to risk the wrath of His Majesty's Secret Service by publishing if he could pin it down firmly.

"Do the police know this?"

Johnson shrugged. "I don't know what they know, but I have another bit of news for you at no extra charge," Johnson said. "I knew Willie Powers. When he was a lad, he belonged to the criminal gang headed by the late lamented Professor James Moriarty."

That caught Hale's full attention, driving Madame Sosostris completely out of his mind. "You mean Moriarty employed children, like Fagin?"

Johnson nodded. "So did Sherlock Holmes, if you remember. He called them his Baker Street irregulars. The professor never bothered with a name."

Hale's mind was racing ahead. He didn't even stop to speculate how Shinwell Johnson knew so much about the long-departed Napoleon of Crime. Evoking his evil memory immediately made Hale think of Tom Eliot's notion of a crime lord, presumably a latter-day Moriarty, out to eliminate the competition. If Eliot were here, he might even suggest that this hypothetical mobster was wiping out the last of Moriarty's minions.

Hale wasn't so sure, but something else Johnson had said gave him an idea—the name Sherlock Holmes.

"Dr. Watson is taking an interest in these Hangman murders," he told Johnson. "Maybe his old friend Holmes is, too."

"Mr. Holmes is retired."

"That's what they say. But I bet his mind isn't retired."

Despite what Sadie seemed to think, Hale didn't see himself as some kind of sleuth who expected to solve the murders himself. He was just a reporter looking for a story. And what a story it would be if he could get Sherlock Holmes himself to comment on the case!

"What do you have in mind?" Johnson asked.

"I'd like to pay him a visit."

Johnson shook his head lugubriously. "I don't think he'd like that. He keeps bees, you know, down in Sussex. The doctor hasn't published a story about him in *The Strand* for three years now, and I expect the latest story was called 'His Last Bow' for a reason."

"Well, perhaps he can be persuaded to make a curtain call. Do you know where—"

Hale stopped cold, almost unable to believe his eyes. Sadie was coming out of the Alhambra, walking quickly down Charing Cross Road with a saucy swing in her step. The red sleeveless dress fell to just a couple of inches below the knee and the loose fitting waist let the dress flow with her every movement. A wide brimmed red hat, T-bar shoes, and silk stockings completed an outfit that made her look even more wonderful than usual. Hale turned back to Johnson, expecting to quickly finish his inquiry, but the man had vanished as unexpectedly as he had arrived. To Hale's further surprise, Sadie looked around, saw Hale, and walked over to him.

"Been waiting long?" she asked.

"Almost a week. I've been here every night."

"I thought so. That's why I've been going out the front door."

"So why the switch tonight?"

She started walking, slowly. "Bad taste in men, I guess. I've missed you, Enoch. I saw you in the audience tonight."

"You were terrific!"

"Thanks. Who was that gorilla I saw you talking to?"

"That was my tailor."

"Well, he did a good job."

She would notice. Sadie herself was always smashingly dressed. Where did a chorus girl get the dough for so many different wardrobes, all in the latest style, and silk stockings? Artificial silk had been on the market for a decade, coming out of the States, but real silk like this took money. There was more to the lovely Sadie Briggs than met the eye. Maybe that was the mystery Hale should be concentrating on.

"Are you still playing detective?" she asked.

Glad as he was to be with Sadie again, Hale couldn't help bristling. *Here we go again.* "I'm still doing my job, if that's what you mean."

"You haven't written about the murders lately. Neither has *The Times*, I noticed. But I saw your last story. You didn't get very much out of that fortune-teller's clients, did you? You only had a quote or two from that Lord Sedgewood."

"He was a bit prickly, but not dangerous. In fact, nobody's even taken a potshot at me yet." Without reopening their argument from Saturday, Hale wanted to make the point that Sadie's fears for his safety had been groundless. For a while he'd been a little nervous about M's boys, but that didn't count. Hale could have regaled Sadie about the eccentricities of Churchill, Shaw, and Yeats, but he thought it was better to move on. "You'll never guess who I'm going to talk to next."

"Lord Carnarvon?"

"No, Sherlock Holmes."

"The detective? You mean he's still alive?"

"He's not even that old—mid-sixties, I think."

Hale told Sadie about his conversation with Johnson.

She bit her lip. "So this Madame Sosostris could have been blackmailing any of her clients. How awful!"

"Yeah, blackmailers are a slimy lot. So that gives some of her clients plenty of reason to kill her, but not the other two victims unless they were just window dressing. It's all pretty confusing for a simple Yank reporter like me. So my idea is to go down to Sussex and get an interview with Holmes. Just getting his thoughts on the case would make a good story, but with luck I might get more. Maybe he actually knows something about Powers and the others because of their criminal backgrounds. At any rate, it certainly won't be dangerous."

"Certainly not. It should be very interesting."

Hale was struck by a sudden thought. "Why don't you come with me?"

He could have sworn that a blush stole over Sadie's fair features. "I'm not that sort of girl, Mr. Hale."

"Well, I am that sort of guy, but that's not what I meant. We'll take the train down and back in the same day. I'll have you back to the Alhambra in the time for your performance."

"But I have to practice for my new solo before that."

She was weakening.

"Call in sick, then have a miraculous recovery when we get back."

She shook her head, but she didn't mean no. "You're leading me astray, Enoch. I hope I don't regret it."

FIFTEEN
On the Sussex Downs

My villa is situated on the southern slope of the downs,
commanding a great view of the Channel.
– "The Adventure of the Lion's Mane"

"Now all I have to do is find out exactly where this
extraordinary beekeeper lives," Hale told Eliot the next
morning. He'd dropped in at his friend's office at 20 King
William Street to let him know about the encounter with
Shinwell Johnson. Eliot shared a room and a typist with a
colleague. The cigarette smoke was thick as London fog.

"I can get that for you," Eliot said cheerfully.

Hale raised his eyebrows. "I was afraid that might be
hard to come by. Isn't that information a bit of a secret, the
great detective's retirement hideaway and all that?"

"There are no secrets from bankers," Eliot said,
"and Mr. Holmes happens to be a client of ours. Lloyds
took over his bank, Capitol & Counties, a couple of years
ago."

"You mean you know him?"

"I wouldn't say that. I work on foreign accounts here in the Colonial and Foreign Department, you know. But I've run into him once or twice. He struck me as a nice enough fellow, and still quite energetic."

Hale shook his head in wonderment. Eliot constantly surprised him, and in new ways each time. Within fifteen minutes Hale had the name of the town and Holmes's villa, The Croft. There was no record of a telephone number, but Hale hadn't planned to call ahead anyway. Reluctant interviewees generally found it easier to say no on the phone.

By pre-arrangement, Hale met Sadie at Charing Cross Station at ten-thirty. She was dressed in bright yellow, shoes to hat, bringing a spot of sunshine to an overcast day.

"You look beautiful for a sick woman," he said.

"I'm not sick, just daft for letting you talk me into this. But the chance to meet the famous Mr. Sherlock Holmes was too good to pass up."

"And I thought you just wanted to make up for lost time with me."

She smiled. "That was a bonus."

A few minutes later their train chugged into the station. Just as they were about to step into a car, Sadie leaned over and spoke into Hale's ear. "I think that man is following you."

He looked around. The platform was crowded. "Which one?"

"The tall one with the long black beard. He's had his eyes on you ever since you greeted me. And now he's rushing to buy a ticket."

Hale smiled. "I think you've been reading too many mystery novels. He was probably just admiring my suit."

The train ride would take an hour and a half on the main line and another half hour on a connecting train out of Brighton to the small village of their destination. It would after twelve-thirty by the time they arrived. But the time passed delightfully for Hale as they talked about Prohibition (passed in the U.S. and turned down in Scotland), the upcoming American presidential election, the latest fashions from Paris, Joan of Arc, women's suffrage, and the high rate of unemployment in England. Sadie's wide green eyes glowed as she talked about the rehearsals for her solo, and narrowed a bit as the subject rolled around once again to Hale's interviews of Madame Sososstris's clients.

"What was Mr. Shaw like?" she asked.

"A lot like Churchill, but with a beard. They both think a little too much of themselves as far as I'm concerned, and I suspect they don't think much of each other."

"And how about Lord Sedgewood?"

"He's just your average lord, I suppose."

"Have you met a lot of lords?" She asked the question as if she knew the answer. She was playing with him.

"No, but I did go to Yale."

Sadie's curiosity about Edward Bridgewater, Lord Sedgewood, exceeded his own. He quickly changed the subject and the train soon pulled into the station at the small East Sussex village that Sherlock Holmes now called home. Hale and Sadie were the only ones who got off.

"See?" he said. "No bearded man, just us."

"That would be too conspicuous. Maybe he's going to get off at the next station and take a cab back."

Hale laughed, and immediately hoped he didn't sound condescending. "You definitely shouldn't be reading mystery novels. You should be writing them."

A ruddy-faced clerk with thick glasses at the station directed them to The Croft, about half a mile away. "Be careful you don't get stung," he said.

"That sounds like good advice," Sadie said as she took Hale's arm and they set off down the village road. It was a sunny day in East Sussex, perfect for a walk in the country.

The Croft was a two-story house made of flintstone and brick. Hale could readily see why someone might want to retreat from crowded, foggy London to this villa with a view of the English Channel. From the angle at which they approached, Hale could see beehives in the back. "This must be the place," he said.

He knocked on the door, repeatedly.

"Maybe he doesn't open the door for strangers," Sadie suggested.

"More likely he's not home." Hale didn't try to hide his disappointment. "I don't see any signs of life."

"Let's ask at the pub. It's not too early for a pint."

The British never thought it was too early for a pint, in Hale's experience.

The Tiger Inn was only about eighty yards away, a whitewashed stone building with a red clay roof. It probably hadn't changed much in the last five hundred years. It was cool inside, rustic, with wood walls and a huge fireplace that must have been a delight in mid-winter. Three locals sat at the bar. All three heads turned toward Hale and Sadie as the newcomers entered. The oldest, with a broad face and a boxer's nose, tipped his cap. Hale didn't think the courtesy was directed at him, but he nodded in the trio's general direction as he approached the bar.

"Two pints of your best bitter, please," he said to the barman, "and another round of whatever these gentlemen are having." The young fellow, who seemed wise in beer beyond his years, served up the pints with no wasted motion and no wasted words.

Hale and Sadie raised their glasses in a silent toast to the occupants of the other stools. The men responded in kind with murmured thanks. After a long, appreciative draught, Hale set his glass down with a thud.

"Would any of you happen to know Mr. Holmes? He lives at The Croft."

The men laughed.

"I suppose you would know him, wouldn't you?" Sadie said. "We were hoping to talk to him, but he doesn't seem to be home."

"Mr. Holmes is retired," said the tall, thin, dark one with a moody face.

Hale wondered whether he and Sadie looked like would-be clients who had taken themselves off to East Sussex in a desperate bid to get the help of the world's still most famous consulting detective.

"He doesn't get many visitors these days," added the third man, an athletic sort with a powerful body despite his gray hair and the face of a scholar.

Hale introduced himself and Sadie, explaining that he was a journalist. The locals were named Herman Patterson, Ian Murdoch, and Harold Sackhurst.

"I was hoping he would talk to us about a series of murders," Hale said. "Maybe we should wait for him."

"He's been gone for a few days," said Sackhurst, the one Hale had sized up as the athlete-scholar. "He's been gone a lot lately."

"On holiday, is he?" Sadie asked.

"He's been going up to London to see his publisher about a new edition of his bee book," said Murdoch, the dark and gloomy one. "Bees are his business now."

Hale sighed. At least Sadie would be back at the Alhambra in plenty of time for tonight's show. He gave each of the three men a business card. "I would be much obliged if you'd give Mr. Holmes my card when you see him and ask him to ring me."

"That we can do," Stackhurst said. He fingered the card thoughtfully. "I believe that Mr. Holmes used to find the Press useful at times, back when he was in the sleuthing line."

Hale and Sadie left a short while later, after drawing out of Stackhurst and Murdock the harrowing tale of a killing on the beach solved by Holmes some years before. Relaxed by the bitter and the conversation, they didn't see the Tiger Inn's third stranger of the day slip into the pub behind them as they headed for the train station. He was a tall man with a beard.

SIXTEEN
Back to Baker Street

"Surely that is Baker Street," I answered, staring
through the dim window.
       – "The Adventure of the Empty House"

Earlier that day the man who had been known as
Captain Basil, Sigerson, Altamont, Escott, and a score of
other names walked slowly down Baker Street. His
imagination, always a much under-appreciated quality in a
detective, took him back to the days when the thoroughfare
was crowded with hansom cabs and lit by gas lamps.

Sherlock Holmes took out a pipe—straight, not
curved—and paused in front of Camden House to cast his
gray eyes at the building across the street with the number
221B on the transom. He looked up at the window of his
old sitting room, the window where a wax bust of him
fashioned by the late Oscar Meunier, of Grenoble, had lured
the great game hunger Colonel Sebastian Moran into the
trap that proved his undoing.

What curious adventures had begun in that little
sitting room! Like a moving picture in his head he could see
with his mind's eye Henry Baker's battered billycock, Dr.
Mortimer's cane, and Thorneycroft Huxtable, M.A., Ph.D,

etc., collapsing on the bearskin hearthrug in utter exhaustion. He smiled as he recalled Grimesby Roylott's attempt to impress him by bending a fireplace poker, which he then had to straighten out to make it useable again.

And then there were the Scotland Yarders who had come through the door to that room, seeking help and usually loath to admit it—Lestrade, Gregson, Bradstreet, Hopkins, and a few others. He'd always had great faith in Hopkins. His rise to the top hadn't surprised Holmes at all.

Greeting them all was Mrs. Hudson, his dear landlady. What she'd put up with, and without complaint! She had suffered almost as much as the good Watson from his strange habits. He had come and gone at irregular hours, shot up the walls, and performed the most malodorous chemical experiments imaginable. And his sudden return from the dead had almost stopped her loving heart. But at least he had always paid the rent on time.

Well, enough of the past, Holmes thought. He had work to do, and not with bees. As in those days long gone, crime was on his mind.

William Powers had been a mediocre entertainer, lacking the flare for showmanship that one would have expected from the "British Houdini." But he was highly skilled at getting out of locked boxes, and even more adept at getting into the locked homes of wealthy individuals. Scotland Yard had finally begun to suspect this, but justice was elusive until it came at the end of the self-appointed Hangman's rope.

Mary Fogarty, wisely rechristening herself with the more evocative name of Madame Sosostris, had been among the most famous clairvoyants on Air Street. How many of her well-heeled clients in government, theater, and literature had she blackmailed? That was impossible to say with certainty. But, according to his old friend Porky Shinwell, the number was not small. Even now Scotland Yard didn't know about Madame's sideline. Her victims didn't talk. They must be living in a great deal of agonizing suspense now, wondering whether their secrets were safe or they had just traded one blackmailer for another, perhaps even harsher.

Of all the criminal classes, Holmes hated blackmailers most of all. He had observed with a great deal of satisfaction as the wife of a nobleman and statesman had emptied a revolver into the odious Charles Augustus Milverton from two feet away. Under the law, he and Watson had been accessories after the fact by not reporting what they had seen. This had never troubled the conscience of Sherlock Holmes in the slightest. The poor woman was dead now, which had given Watson the freedom to write about the case.

James Alcock had been a forger and counterfeiter of exceptional talent. It was only circumstantial evidence and the unsubstantiated word of men who were themselves criminals that put him in Scotland Yard's sights. But it seemed the printing press was not the only tool he used in criminal activities. Alcock and his associates may have been in some deep waters indeed, bringing him into brother Mycroft's sphere of activity—if the word "activity" could ever be properly applied to his languorous older brother.

Mycroft was to be avoided in this affair, but that would not be easy.

There were too many cooks in this soup. Mycroft and his men, Wiggins, Langdale Pike, Porky Shinwell, and that American reporter, Hale—their involvement was going to make his job much harder.

He smiled. With all those pieces on the chessboard they certainly didn't need another knight in the form of Sherlock Holmes. A pawn would do the trick—someone so insignificant as to not be noticed and yet capable of taking the queen.

For years he had maintained five small refuges in London where he could slip in as Holmes and emerge as someone else. Even Watson didn't know that in his supposed retirement he still maintained a flat for that purpose, rented under the fanciful name of Ormond Sacker. The hideaway was where it would be least expected, because it was so obvious.

Sherlock Holmes crossed the street and entered his old quarters at 221B.

SEVENTEEN
"Good Afternoon, Mr. Bond"

Is it perfume from a dress
That makes me so digress?
    – T.S. Eliot, "The Love Song of J. Alfred
    Prufrock"

"Well, that was disappointing," Sadie sighed as they settled into the train car. "The closest I got to meeting Sherlock Holmes was a good view of his beehives."

"At least you didn't get stung," Hale said. "Journalism is like that sometimes. I guess detective work is pretty much the same thing. You hit a lot of dead ends before you hit pay dirt. The trick is to not give up."

"No, I can't see you giving up."

Hale closed his eyes and enjoyed the closeness of Sadie and the smell of her perfume.

"So what do we do next?" she asked.

He opened one eye. "You have a show. That's what's next for you, young lady. I'll drop you off, and then pick you up afterwards for some drinks at Murray's. It will be a perfect Friday night."

"No, silly, I mean, where do we go with the murders?"

She'd changed her tune faster than a Victrola at a dance party, from trying to talk him out of reporting on the Hangman murders to talking about "we" investigating the same. Hale didn't know what to make of that.

"Shinwell Johnson said a couple of interesting things worth following up. I intend to ask Wiggins if he knew that Madame Sosostris was a blackmailer and that William Powers had once been a member or the Moriarty gang. I think it's about time to write another story, no matter what the consequences."

Sadie pulled away, her body stiffening. "What do you mean 'the consequences'? What haven't you been telling me, Enoch?"

He put up his hands. "It's nothing that dramatic. Certain people in His Majesty's government made it clear that they didn't welcome me sticking my Yankee nose into a business that could involve official secrets."

"Then what you're doing *is* dangerous!"

"I said the government, not the camorra or the Black Hand! It's not like they're going to kill me. The most they would do is throw me in jail for a little while. Besides, I don't think the stuff I'm poking into is what they're worried about."

"What *are* they worried about?"

"If I knew that, my dear, I'd really be in big trouble."

It was late afternoon by the time they arrived at the Alhambra. Sadie left Hale at the back door with a lingering kiss.

"I like the smooch much better that way—without the slap afterward," he said. "Break a leg. I'll be waiting here after the show."

"Don't *you* break anything. And stay out of trouble."

He held up three fingers. "Scout's honor!"

Hale had never been a Scout.

He was just turning to leave when out of the corner of his eye he caught a glimpse of a tall figure coming out of the Alhambra. It looked like . . . yes, it was.

"Good afternoon, Mr. Bond," he called.

Commander Ian Bond started, then put a bland look on his face. "Mr. Hale, isn't it?" he said in his Scottish burr. He was dressed in a lightweight business suit, blue, but Hale imagined the naval officer looking right at home in a kilt.

"That's right. I'm surprised you remember me, Commander, considering how fast you ran away from me at Alcock's." The title was just to let the Scot know that Hale wasn't totally in the dark.

"I still have nothing to say to the Press." He began to walk briskly away.

Hale walked just as fast. "Were you at the Alhambra just now because it was the scene of the first Hangman murder?"

That stopped Bond in his tracks. "What the devil gave you that idea?"

"Not what, who. A mutual friend of ours with a name so short it only has one letter suggested that you might look into the murders."

"I'm a military man, not a detective."

"Can I quote you on that?"

"It wouldn't be a good idea to quote me on anything, Mr. Hale. In fact, I think you would regret it very deeply."

"Is that a threat?"

Bond shot Hale a humorless smile and resumed walking. This time Hale stood where he was. He knew a brick wall when he ran into one. He turned around, almost smacking into an elderly man, bent, with frayed clothes and a crooked smile.

108

"Flowers for your girl, sir?" The Cockney accent was so thick that Hale could barely understand it. The old man held up a bundle of roses.

"How much?"

Hale dug into his pockets and gave the poor fellow more than he was asking for. He felt a bit sorry for him. He had such intelligent gray eyes.

EIGHTEEN
A Startling Suggestion

"It is the first quality of a criminal investigator that he
should see through a disguise."
– Sherlock Holmes, *The Hound of the Baskervilles*

"Keep trying to find Holmes," Nigel Rathbone said.
"'Famous Detective's Theory on Hangman Murders' would
make a great headline, no matter how long it takes you to
get the story. Meanwhile, let's go with what you got from
that Johnson character about Fogarty and Powers. That's
the story I want to see next. But talk to Wiggins first. I want
an official Scotland Yard comment on the news that this so-
called clairvoyant was a blackmailer and that Powers was
once part of the Moriarty gang."

The fast-talking South African didn't actually rub his
hands together with satisfaction, but that was the mood he
conveyed.

Rathbone was sitting on Hale's desk in the
newsroom of the Central News Syndicate. It was late
Saturday morning, the day after Hale's unsuccessful foray to

the South Downs. A few reporters and sub-editors were at work around them. Hale smoked a panatela in his chair while Rathbone sucked on a pipe.

"So you're not worried about the Official Secrets Act?" Hale asked.

"The further we get away from your visit to Pall Mall, the less that bothers me, Hale. If His Majesty's Secret Service was that worried, they'd have taken some other action against you by now."

"You mean like having somebody follow me?"

Rathbone regarded his reporter shrewdly. "Why do you say that?"

Why had he? "Just a stray thought, I guess. Sadie— that's my young lady—had this wild idea that a man with a black beard was following me when we got on the train at Charing Cross Station. But we were the only ones who got off the train at our destination."

"A beard could easily be a disguise to prevent you from recognizing the man," Rathbone mused. "If he really was following you, I mean."

"Sherlock Holmes was an expert on disguises," came a familiar voice from two desks away. The ancient Horace Harker, retired but unrestrained, had been eavesdropping. He stood up. "I met him once, you know, years ago. I helped him solve that business of the six Napoleons."

"Yes, we've all heard that story several times," Rathbone said, patently struggling to maintain his patience. Besides being boring and repetitive, everybody at CNS knew that Harker's version of the story omitted a key detail that changed everything. Harker had played an important role in the case, all right, but that role was as a dupe. Sherlock Holmes, by way of his friend Inspector Lestrade, had fed Harker false information as to what Holmes and the Yard had concluded about the case. Harker had written that misinformation into a news report. The killer, as hoped, was lulled by the story into a false sense of security that allowed Holmes to trap him.

"Holmes should be your chief suspect, you know," Harker said.

"What are you babbling out?" Rathbone snapped.

The old journalist looked hurt. "I was just stating the obvious. I've heard you talking—more than you might think. The idea that the Hangman is a vigilante, somebody taking the law into his own hands, makes plenty of sense to me. Well, gentlemen, there never was such a man for doing that as Sherlock Holmes. He let thieves and murderers off scot-free on a promise that they would reform, he knew the identity of Charles Augustus Milverton's killer but didn't report it, and he even resorted to burglary himself. And that's just what's been recorded in Dr. Watson's accounts of his cases. God only knows what his accomplice has been hiding from the public."

Rathbone's normally pale complexion began to turn red. Hale was almost certain he was about to bark "Nonsense!" or something of the sort.

Hale was not so sure, however. Holmes had been in London a lot recently, according to his friends at the Tiger Inn. Had he been to town on the dates that Powers, Sosostris, and Alcock had been killed? That would be worth checking into. And did Holmes know that Madame Sosostris had been a blackmailer, perhaps with her tentacles into some of the most powerful men in the country? Shinwell Johnson had known that, and Eliot had said that he was an old associate of Holmes.

All of this raced through Hale's mind before Rathbone even had a chance to open his mouth in response to Harker's startling suggestion. And Rathbone never did have that chance—because the phone on Hale's desk rang, making all of them jump. Hale lunged for it.

"Hello, this is Enoch Hale at the Central News Syndicate."

"It's Wiggins. The Hangman has been busy again. You'll want to get over here right away."

Hale gripped the phone. "Where are you?"

"At Islington Studios. The latest victim is Rory O'Quinn, the moving picture actor."

NINETEEN
Murder on the Set

There will be time to murder and create . . .
  – T.S. Eliot, "The Love Song of J. Alfred
  Prufrock"

Although Rory O'Quinn was not a major star or a
household name, the Irish-American actor had been steadily
building a solid reputation for himself. First on stage and
then in moving pictures, he had received good reviews for a
series of second-billing performances. Hale had seen two of
his films, *The Picture of Dorian Gray* and *Raffles*.

"This time his name was going to go on top,"
Wiggins said as they stood over the body.

"It still is," Hale said, "only in newspaper headlines
instead of theater marquees."

O'Quinn had landed the part of John Vansittart
Smith in a film version of *The Ring of Thoth*, based on an
Arthur Conan Doyle short story that had appeared in *The
Cornhill* magazine in 1890. Although the story was thirty
years old, its tale of an Egyptian mummy and her faithful

lover was expected to be popular with modern audiences fascinated by all the discoveries in Egypt of late.

In the original story, the perpetual student Vansittart Smith was little more than an observer to a 4,000-year-old love triangle involving an Egyptian governor's daughter and the two men who loved her. In the film script, though, he had been transformed into a considerably more active character.

"So this is supposed to be the Egyptian section of the Louvre?" Hale looked around the movie set with its papier-mâché statues and its perfectly wrapped mummies. "It doesn't exactly look like it." He knew that because he'd seen the real thing.

"Close enough for moving pictures, I expect," Wiggins drawled.

O'Quinn had been a handsome man, with a firm jawline just made for cowboy pictures. But he was older and shorter than he looked on the screen, in his late thirties and about five-foot-six. His body had been cut down from a rope tied to a steel rafter.

Famous Players–Lasky Corporation, an American moving picture outfit, had taken over the derelict power station of the Metropolitan Electric Supply Co. in the borough of Islington, gutted it, and built two large studios. The whole building now had the benefit of artificial light, thanks to a special cable bringing electricity a mile and a half from Shoreditch. Hale and Wiggins were standing by the body in the second studio, which was located on what the British called the first floor.

"I'm getting a premonition, Wiggins." Hale put his hands over his eyes like a music hall psychic. "My sixth sense tells me that Rory O'Quinn had a criminal past, or maybe even a criminal present, but the police of two continents could never prove it."

Wiggins shook his head. "Not a whiff of it. We haven't been able to contact the States yet, of course, but he hadn't come to our attention as a bent one."

"Did you know that Madame Sosostris had a sideline in blackmail?"

"What?"

Hale told Wiggins what he'd learned from Shinwell Johnson. It was all news to the chief inspector. "That's not to say I'm surprised and shocked," he added.

"So maybe O'Quinn was up to some dirty deeds you didn't know about either," Hale said.

"I won't say that couldn't be so."

And yet, it did seem unlikely that a moving picture actor whose career was on the rise would be involved in something dodgy, unless it was in his past. Maybe O'Quinn had committed a crime as a young man and wound up as one of the Madame's blackmail victims. But why would someone kill both her and a man she was blackmailing? It made no sense. By now, however, imagining possible connections among the Hangman's victims had become a habit for Hale, practically uncontrollable.

"Thanks for calling me, Wiggins," Hale said. "Not many coppers would want the Press around for the fourth murder in a series you haven't been able to crack."

Wiggins winced. "Maybe I'm just stupid. But a great detective once said the Press is a most valuable institution if only you know how to use it. I'm hoping that your stories will bring forth somebody who saw something."

Clearly Chief Inspector Wiggins and the man known as M had quite different philosophies regarding his reporting of the Hangman murders.

"I take it that nobody happened to see O'Quinn's killer leaving the set?"

"We're just getting started with our inquiries. Ruby Alexander found the body about three hours ago. They had an early call, but O'Quinn got to the set before anybody else—except his killer. I was told that Miss Alexander practically needed a fainting couch, she was so upset."

Miss Alexander was still a major star, as she had been since the beginning of cinema. Her casting as the tragic heroine Atma, however, had drawn some catcalls from critics. Charitably put, she could be described as a bit long in the tooth for the part. She was at least a decade older than the two actors vying for her favor in the film—John Thane as Sostra, the unfortunate son of the chief priest of Osiris in the great temple of Abaris, and Robert Craig as Parmes, the young priest of Thoth.

"This is terrible! Terrible! We've only shot half of Rory's lines!"

Apparently Cedric Pinkwater, one of the pioneering directors of the British moving picture industry, had a penchant for dramatic entrances. He walked onto the set of faux sarcophagi shouting and flapping his arms, a florid-faced stout man with his thinning hair combed straight back off of his high forehead. He wore a white silk scarf at his throat and a pink rose on the lapel of his green blazer.

"I'm sure Mr. O'Quinn is very sorry about that," Wiggins said.

Pinkwater scowled. "And just who are you, smart mouth?"

"Chief Inspector Henry Wiggins, sir. And this is Mr. Enoch Hale of the Central Press Syndicate."

"Coppers! Reporters! What next—labor unionists and Irish rebels?" The director stopped, struck by a thought. "Well, I suppose there's no such thing as bad publicity. All this Press coverage should give the film a boost, if I can figure out a way to finish it. I know! Vansittart Smith gets murdered halfway through the picture. Art imitates life! People will flock to see that. I'll get my screenwriter on it right away."

Hale worked hard at keeping his features neutral so as to conceal the instant dislike he felt for this bombastic tyrant of the movie set.

"I take it you can shed no light on this tragedy," Wiggins said.

"Eh? Oh, I just got here. Ruby found the body."

"Yes, we know. But I was wondering whether Mr. O'Quinn might have said anything unusual or acted strangely in the past several days."

"Hmm. Well, now that you mention it, he did seem a little distracted. He was having trouble following direction. And once, when a member of the stage crew dropped a hammer, I thought he was going to have a heart attack. But actors are a strange lot at best. What does that have to do with the murder?"

"That remains to be seen. You probably realize that this is just the latest in a series of murders by hanging. We're not quite sure of the connection between all of the victims, but we feel certain there was one. The killer may have been somebody Mr. O'Quinn knew, but probably wasn't one of the other actors or a member of the crew. Have you noticed any strangers on the scene of late?"

Pinkwater raised his arms and looked about. "On a movie set? Are you daft? People are in and out all day long and I don't know half of them. And I'm supposed to be in charge!"

"That means the killer has no particular reason to make himself scarce," Hale said. "Maybe he's still around."

"That's not a completely mad notion," Wiggins said, as if making a great concession. "Care to give us a look around, Mr. Pinkwater?"

The director shrugged his shoulders. "Why not? I can see we're not going to get much work done today anyway."

The floor they were on was set up so that as many as six scenes could be set and filmed simultaneously for speed and efficiency of production. The trio walked through the Egyptian exhibit at the Louvre, the great temple of Abaris, an ancient pyramid, and a private club in London within ten minutes.

"For some strange reason," Pinkwater said, "the London County Council classifies the building as a theater, not a factory, so we had to build each studio with two fire escapes."

Hale made a note. The killer had at least two options for leaving the murder scene. Strange that British law considered theatergoers as more worthy of protection than factory workers.

Overlooking the first-floor studio were some of the principle dressing rooms and the offices of the art director. "We have other dressing rooms on the floor above and in the basement," Pinkwater said. "In fact, three hundred people can dress for a production at the same time downstairs."

"That should come in handy when you film the Book of Exodus," Hale equipped.

"Rumor has it that DeMille is working on that, but I hear he's years away from going into production."

They were walking past the art director's office when a pudgy, balding fellow about Hale's age and a head shorter came out.

"Oh, hello, Hitch," Pinkwater said in a desultory fashion.

"Sir." Hitch bowed—comically, Hale thought, although he wasn't sure whether or not Hitch intended it that way.

Pinkwater turned to Wiggins and Hale. "Hitch here designs title cards, but he harbors a not-so-secret desire to be a director. I suppose you heard about our murder, Hitch?"

"Yes, sir. A very shocking turn of events."

The man talked slowly, enunciating each word. He was hardly an impressive figure. If the idea of "talkies" like Sarah Bernhardt's *Le Duel d'Hamlet* ever caught on, he would be out of a job and perhaps out of the business. It was hard to believe that he would ever have the commanding presence of a director, however much that might be the fellow's fantasy.

"Mr. Hitch—"

"Hitchcock, sir," the man interrupted Wiggins.

"Mr. Hitchcock, did you see or hear anything unusual over the past several hours?"

"No, I don't believe I— Oh! I just remembered. I did see someone I didn't know come out of the Louvre set a few hours ago. He seemed to be in a hurry, head down, and almost ran into me."

"That could have been just before the body was found," Hale said, "which means he was most likely the murderer."

"What did he look like?" Wiggins asked.

"He was a tall fellow, but I couldn't see much of his face. It was covered by a dark beard."

TWENTY
Profile of a Sleuth

"It is always a joy to meet an American . . ."
 – Sherlock Holmes, "The Adventure of the
 Noble Bachelor"

"Thank you, Mr. Hitchcock," Wiggins said. "That could prove very helpful indeed."

The man had been tall, according to Hitchcock. Well, the bearded man who had followed Hale and Sadie— if indeed he had—wasn't particularly tall. But Hitch was only about five-six, so his concept of tall may have been a bit skewed. At any rate, the description of the intruder seemed to put paid to Horace Harker's suggestion that Sherlock Holmes was the killer.

Pinkwater continued the tour of the Islington Studios, showing off the ground-floor studio like a proud parent.

"Here we have the scene dock." He pointed at a messy area of paint and canvas. A veteran of amateur theater productions at Yale, Hale was a bit surprised to find that moving picture backgrounds weren't all that much different from the painted scenery in a play. "When they've been painted they can go directly to this studio or by elevator to the one upstairs," Pinkwater said.

"Don't you worry about the fog getting inside?" Hale said. "I've heard that's a problem for London studios."

Pinkwater chuckled. "I was hoping you'd ask that. It may be a problem over at Hepworth Studios, but not here. We've installed an ingenious system of high-pressure and low-pressure pipes to deal with that. If the fog gets in, it's forced to the center and expelled from the roof. I was a bit skeptical myself at first, but it actually works. Now, here's the most unique part of the studio."

Only with great effort did Hale resist the impulse to tell the little martinet that the word "unique" is unique in that it can't be modified. If something is unique, it can't be most unique. It's just unique. But Hale didn't think Pinkwater would appreciate being told that.

The director was pointing to a huge water tank sunk into the middle of the floor. "We can shoot water scenes there. We've even put windows into the sides of the tank so that we can capture underwater action. Hullo, who the hell is that?"

From the other end of a large room, on the same side of the tank, a tall, bird-like figure walked their way, his head apparently sunk in thought. He was over six feet tall, although somewhat bowed with age, and lean. A great hawk's bill of a nose dominated his face. With a start, Hale suddenly realized that he was looking at one of the most famous profiles in the world.

Wiggins's face lit up. "Why it's—"

"William Gillette," the man announced.

122

Pinkwater marched toward the figure, his hand outstretched. "We've never met, Mr. Gillette, but I'd know you anywhere!"

Indeed, who wouldn't? William Gillette was one of America's greatest actors, both on stage and in moving pictures. Although he had written and starred in many other plays, he was best known for portraying the man Hale had first believed he was looking at—Sherlock Holmes. The man looked remarkably like the Frederic Dorr Steele drawings of Holmes that illustrated Dr. Watson's accounts in *Collier's* magazine. Gillette had been playing Holmes for more than twenty years in his melodrama *Sherlock Holmes*, which had been made into a moving picture by Essanay Studios just four years ago.

Too bad he isn't the real thing, Hale thought. We could use Sherlock Holmes on this case more than ever.

"Yes, I'm Gillette," the actor said in a most definitely American accent. "Mr. Pinkwater, I presume?" He shook hands with the director. "I found myself in the neighborhood and decided to visit your studios that I've heard so much about. The guard recognized me and let me in. I hope you don't mind."

"Not at all. We're honored to have you. In fact, we were hoping you'd drop by later for some of the shooting on *Held By the Enemy*."

It had been one of Gillette's most successful plays, the one that had thrust him into stardom years before *Sherlock Holmes*.

"Thank you, but I suspect that you have something more serious on your mind right now, judging by the Metropolitan Police cars outside." He turned to Wiggins. "From that British Bulldog whose outline I can see in the outside right pocket of your overcoat and the handcuffs in your back pocket, I presume that one of those cars is yours."

123

"There's been a murder," the chief inspector said. "Yes, I'm from the Yard. My name is Wiggins and this is Mr. Enoch Hale, a fellow countryman of yours from the Central Press Syndicate."

Pinkwater burst in with the thirty-second version of what had happened.

"Well, well," Gillette said. "I have to admit that I've never been near a murder in real life. May I see the body, Chief Inspector?"

Wiggins rubbed his chin—a bit dramatically, Hale thought. "I suppose if you don't get too close it won't do any harm. The Press has already been on the scene."

They took the elevator back up to the first floor. Inspector Cloud and Constable Gale were still in the studio, along with a man that Hale presumed to be a police doctor. The fatal rope still hung from the rafters. Gillette noticed it right away.

"I've only been in England a short time," he said, "but I've seen headlines about the co-called 'Hangman murders.' Is this another one?"

Wiggins nodded. "Nothing surer."

Gillette knelt down on all fours for a close look at the corpse. "The victim was an actor, I see."

"How did you know that?" Hale asked.

As the part called for, O'Quinn had been dressed in the everyday clothes of a modern scholar, not ancient Egyptian regalia.

"He's wearing makeup," Gillette said. "It takes a lot of people with a lot of different skills to make a moving picture, but only the actors wear makeup."

"Always did his own," Pinkwater said. "He insisted on it."

Hale regarded Gillette with respect. "You really have that deduction thing down pat, don't you?"

124

Gillette stood up. "People expect it of Sherlock Holmes, I'm afraid. It's really quite simple if one tries. I don't know why Watson made so much of it. For example, Mr. Hale, it's quite obvious that you come from a family of means, disappointed but not disaffected by your choice of profession."

"Good guess."

"I never guess. I've also never met a journalist who wears Brooks Brothers suits. That takes more money than Fleet Street pays out, until you're the boss, if then. Your family can hardly be pleased that you've become a scribbler, which may explain why you're pursuing that trade in old England instead of the New England your accent comes from. Yet it's obvious that they haven't cut off your allowance since you're wearing the very latest style and a new fabric that Brooks Brothers has just begun to import from India called Madras. By the way, that notebook in your hand is as indicative of your profession as Chief Inspector Wiggins's two-and-a-half inch barrel weapon and handcuffs are of his."

As Gillette had said, that didn't seem to Hale nearly so difficult or so impressive now that he'd explained it. Something about the actor was bothering Hale, something that he'd said or done, but Hale just couldn't put his metaphorical finger on it.

Gillette turned to Wiggins. "What's your operating theory behind these Hangman murders?"

"We don't think these are just random killings." Wiggins displayed more patience with the actor's inquisitiveness than Hale would have expected. Perhaps the Scotland Yarder was mesmerized by Gillette's fame. "The killer has gone to too much trouble when he could have just pulled somebody off the street if he had a mad hankering to kill just anybody. So there must be some link among the victims, and we're trying to find it. Up to now, they all had a suspected life of crime that the Yard couldn't prove. But

O'Quinn breaks that pattern. So far as we know, he's clean."

Gillette walked over to one of the fire escapes, and then back again. He walked around the set, musing aloud. "O'Quinn is in makeup, ready to begin the day's shooting. He arrives first on the set—except for his killer, who is waiting for him, perhaps hiding behind one of these papier-mâché statues of rather ostentatious Egyptian gods. Judging by the bruises on the corpse's neck, I believe the killer attacked O'Quinn from behind and strangled him with his hands before he put the rope around him."

"Strangled!" Pinkwater exclaimed. "Then why go to all the trouble to hang the man if he was already dead or dying?"

"Because the gentlemen of the Press don't call these the 'Hangman murders' for nothing," Gillette said dryly. "The point of the rope isn't just to kill, it's to send a message. In the killer's mind, his victims weren't murdered—they were executed."

Gillette was a quick study, Hale thought.

Pinkwater chuckled. "I guess we don't need the real Sherlock Holmes with you around, Mr. Gillette."

"I can but try."

"Would you like to talk to Ruby Alexander?" the director asked. "She found the body. You must be old friends. Didn't she play Alice Faulkner when you came to London with *Sherlock Holmes* about twenty years ago?"

Hale wouldn't have noticed Gillette's wince if he hadn't been watching the actor closely. "I don't think that will be necessary, unless she happened to see the killer leave the scene. She didn't? I didn't think so. Well, we have the body itself, which is the most powerful witness we could have. How unfortunate that the official police have been all over the scene, and the Press as well. However, you did

126

manage to avoid obliterating a few of the killer's footprints in the dust."

While storm clouds gathered on Wiggins's countenance, Hale repressed a snigger. It was as plain as the nose on Gillette's face that he was avoiding Ruby Alexander. Either they hadn't gotten along when they worked together on stage all those years ago . . . or they'd gotten along entirely too well.

"I examined the floor myself," Wiggins sputtered. "It's full of footprints, dozens of them! How could you possibly . . ."

"The square-toed boots are quite unmistakable. They belong to a man about six foot-one, judging by his stride."

"Okay," Hale said, "but how do you know that they belong to the killer?"

Gillette pointed to the fire escape that he had gone to earlier. "Because the footprints come from there. The killer climbed up the fire escape and in that window, and then simply walked away after the murder."

"But not unseen," Wiggins said.

Gillette made a question mark of his face.

"It's true that Miss Alexander didn't see the killer leave," Wiggins said, "but you didn't give me a chance to say that someone else did. At least, we think so."

"It was one of my men," Pinkwater said, in a self-important way that suggested it was his own personal achievement. "He saw a man with a beard leaving right before Ruby screamed, a man he'd never seen before."

Gillette closed his eyes for a moment. Hale suspected that he was silently counting to ten. "Do you mind if I talk to this fellow?"

Within three minutes Hale, Wiggins, Pinkwater, and Gillette were practically crowding Hitchcock out of his tiny office. The little man's eyes opened wide as he saw the invasion coming.

Pinkwater was brusque. "Hitch, this is Mr. William Gillette."

"Of course it is, sir."

"Tell him what you told us earlier about the man you saw leaving the Louvre set this morning."

Hitchcock repeated his story in the same monotone as before, giving the tale of his encounter with the likely murderer about as much romance as the fifth proposition of Euclid.

Gillette asked a rapid-fire series of questions: How tall was the intruder? How did he walk? Did he say anything? ("No, he merely nodded at me.") In which direction did he go?

Hitchcock answered each question with little hesitation, a self-assured witness.

"I just have one more question," Gillette said finally. "That black beard, was it genuine or false?"

"Oh, it was quite false, sir."

TWENTY-ONE
The Man with the Beard

"I was following you, of course."

"Following me? I saw nobody."

"That is what you must expect to see when I am following you," said Sherlock Holmes.

— "The Adventure of the Devil's Foot"

As he left his flat to go for a Sunday morning stroll the next day, Hale was still blaming himself for not asking the right question. In a building full of makeup and costumes, he should have thought of the possibility of disguise. He couldn't blame Hitchcock for not volunteering the information.

But Pinkwater did. Poor Hitch, Hale thought. The director had called him names for five minutes, finding an enormous variety of ways to say that Hitchcock had been stupid for not telling them the beard was phony without being asked. The little man seemed to take the abuse in stride, though. Probably he was used to it. But Hale figured that whatever slight chance that Alfred Hitchcock ever had of advancing in the moving picture business had probably been lost in that encounter.

For his part, Hale had slept little that night. He'd been up reading *The Adventures of Sherlock Holmes*, which he purchased at a book stall that afternoon.

The first edition of the book had come out when Hale was only two years old; the stories in it had appeared as a series in *The Strand Magazine* even earlier. Hale had read the book, and one or two other Holmes case books as well, as a boy. But he barely remembered them now. He certainly had no recollection of Holmes as a kind of vigilante.

He did, however, remember that Holmes was a master of disguise. He could well have been the man in the beard who had followed Hale and was later seen by the hapless Hitchcock.

Reading through the stories at a breakneck pace, skimming some parts, Hale was astonished at what he found. In at least four of the twelve stories, and possibly five, Holmes had set himself above the law in some way. Hale made a chart in his Moleskine notebook listing each such story, the action, and a quote from Sherlock Holmes:

STORY	ACTION	QUOTE
"A Scandal in Bohemia"	attempted theft	"You don't mind breaking the law?"
"The Boscombe Valley Mystery"	lets the murderer escape	". . . your secret, whether you be alive or dead, shall be safe with me."
"The Adventure of the Blue Carbuncle"	lets the thief escape	"I suppose that I am compounding a felony, but it is just possible that I am saving a soul."
"The Adventure of the Speckled Band"	redirects a deadly snake toward the murderer	"I am no doubt indirectly responsible for Dr. Grimesby Roylott's death, and I cannot say that it is likely to weigh very heavily upon my conscience."

In addition, in "The Adventure of the Beryl Coronet," Holmes learns the name of the receiver of stolen goods by promising the thief that there would be no prosecution. Hale wasn't sure whether it was illegal to negotiate with a thief—he presumed that insurance companies did so all the time—but it was certainly not the action of a man who respected the law.

What few hours of the night remained when Hale had finished reading through the book were mostly filled with rolling over in his mind the staggering implications of his research. Could Sherlock Holmes, the great detective admired from Boston to Tibet, really be a mass murderer acting as a vigilante?

Such were Hale's thoughts when he heard his name called behind him on his morning stroll. He turned around to find a sight so unexpected it was hard at first for his brain to process it. About ten yards down the street stood a roughly clothed, bearded man with his hands pinned behind his back by none other than . . . William Gillette! He must have incredible strength for an old man, Hale thought.

"Does this fellow look familiar?" Gillette asked.

Hale nodded. "I could swear that he's the man we saw at Charing Cross Station." He was the right size, not so tall as Hitchcock seemed to think, and the beard was the same spade shape and black color.

Hale quickly crossed the distance between them and pulled on the man's beard.

"Ow! What are you, daft?" Tears streamed down the poor wretch's eyes and his beard remained firmly in place.

"I guess Hitchcock was wrong about the false beard," Hale said. He didn't feel motivated to apologize for the pain caused in the course of this discovery.

"I doubt it," Gillette said. "This isn't the man that Hitchcock saw leaving the studio."

"You mean it's a different bearded man?" This was beginning to feel like a P.G. Wodehouse farce. The only thing missing was the butler. "How do you know?"

Gillette pointed to his captive's boots. "They don't match the footprints. And I sincerely doubt that this poor fellow owns more than one pair of boots. Nor is he tall enough. No, this isn't our killer. But he was following you this morning."

The captive began to struggle. "I were not. And besides, you can't prove it."

"While you were following Mr. Hale, I was following you."

The bearded man looked defiant. "I never seen you behind me."

"No one ever sees me behind them. Your own skills in the fine art of surveillance, on the other hand, are considerably less developed, Mr. John Hawkins."

The man's eyes widened, all attempt at struggle abandoned. "You're Sherlock Holmes!"

"I suppose if I denied it you wouldn't believe me," Gillette said in an excellent British accent.

"How'd you know my name?

"It's on the inside label of your coat. I read it upside down while I was subduing you. More important than that, Mr. Hawkins, who are you working for?"

Hawkins attempted to regain some measure of dignity, straightening his back. "His Majesty the King. I'm a nanny in the royal household."

"That kind of attitude isn't going to do you any damned good," Hale said. "If you don't start cooperating, we'll march you right down to New Scotland Yard."

"Fine! I'll explain that I was minding me own business when you blokes kidnapped me!"

"And who do you think the Metropolitan Police will believe," Gillette said, "you or Sherlock Holmes?"

Maybe he believes he really *is* Holmes, Hale thought. He'd read of such things—actors who got so lost in a role that the line in their minds between acting and reality was erased.

"Aw, come on, give me a break, fellows," Hawkins pleaded. "I'm just a working man and I want to keep working. You could lose me my job."

Hale was moved by the plea, but not Gillette. "You could always go back to blacksmithing."

"How did you—"

"It's a habit of mine. Listen, you won't have a job of any kind if you're in jail. But we needn't tell your employer that you gave up his name. We can say I followed you to his residence. That way, you'll only look incompetent."

"Aye, and no mistake about that," mumbled Hawkins. "All right, all right. I'm Lord Sedgewood's man."

"Sedgewood!" Hale's surprise was total. He had scarcely given the earl a thought since their contentious interview more than a week before. He certainly hadn't thought of him as a serious suspect in the murders.

"Why did he have you following Hale?" Gillette asked.

"Good luck finding that out, mate."

"I don't depend on luck," Gillette said.

TWENTY-TWO
Alias Sadie Briggs

"It is always awkward doing business with an alias."
– Sherlock Holmes, "The Adventure of the Blue
Carbuncle"

"I bet that Madame Sosostris was blackmailing Sedgewood," Hale said as they waited to meet Hawkins at the earl's townhouse. "He must have been worried that I'd find out. That's why he was so hostile to me and that's why he had me followed."

"In my experience, his sort doesn't need a reason to be hostile to their social inferiors," Gillette said dryly, lighting a cigarette. "That includes you, Hale. Despite your prominent and wealthy family, you are a member of the Press—and quite a good one. To tell you the truth, I've taken more than a casual interest in these Hangman murders. I've read all of your stories. They're full of amazing detail."

"Thank you."

"What did you leave out?"

"What do you mean?"

"There must be a story behind the story. Most reporters know more than they print, but that must be especially true for you. You had a series of excellent stories, and then nothing. What didn't you report, and why?"

Something about Gillette inspired trust. Hoping that he wouldn't regret it later, Hale told him all about the mysterious M and the strategy he had worked out with Rathbone to avoid coming up against the Official Secrets Act.

"So you think M has this fellow Bond investigating the murders?"

"He implied it."

It was on the tip of Hale's tongue to tell Gillette about his Harker-inspired suspicion of Sherlock Holmes. He might as well tell the actor everything. But he couldn't bring himself to do it. In the cold light of day, the idea seemed mad.

Gillette smoked meditatively. "Well, this case won't die for lack of attention, what with the Press watching Scotland Yard and the Government watching the Press. At least we have Lord Sedgewood all to ourselves, for whatever that might be worth."

With a further inducement of some cash from Hale's family allowance, Hawkins had agreed to meet them outside the townhouse at Number 10 Carlton Terrace at teatime, when Lord Sedgewood was expecting him to report.

Hawkins was as good as his word. He arrived on time with a hat in his hand and a sour expression on his face. "Let's get this over with, right?"

The maid, a young Irish girl, was suspicious of the trio who appeared at the door. "They're with me," Hawkins said gruffly.

"I'll tell His Lordship," the girl promised dubiously.

A few minutes later she guided them back to the library where Edward Bridgewater, the Earl of Sedgewood, had received Hale on his first visit. The peer was standing at a window, looking outside, when the maid announced them. Sedgewood clearly understood that standing is a power position. He was also telling them, Hale figured, that he was an important man, thinking great thoughts as he gazed out at the metropolis beyond.

Sedgewood turned slowly toward his visitors. But there was nothing slow about his voice. It cracked out like a bullwhip. "What is the meaning of this, Hawkins?"

"It's not his fault," Hale said. "I guess you remember me, Your Lordship, and this is Mr. William Gillette."

The expression on Hawkins's face telegraphed the confusion he must have been feeling. He believed the man was Sherlock Holmes.

"Gillette?" Sedgewood repeated. "The American actor?" Ignoring the contempt in the peer's voice, Gillette nodded slightly in acknowledgement.

"None other," Hale affirmed. "Here's what happened: Mr. Gillette got the idea into his head that this man was following me, and thought it would be a lark to follow him in return. Mr. Gillette was kind enough to let me in on the game when my shadow gave up for the day. I guess your man—Hawkins, you said? —got bored watching my flat while I read the Sunday papers all day. When I realized where he was going, I thought I ought to drop in and say hello, Lord Sedgewood. And by the way, why the *hell* was he following me? I assume that was your doing."

Sedgewood didn't seem to question Hale's fabricated account of what had brought the two unwanted visitors to Carlton Terrace. His pale face flushed. "I don't have to answer that! You're just a damned reporter."

"True enough, Your Lordship," Gillette drawled, "but even earls have to answer to Scotland Yard. Would you rather talk to our friend Chief Inspector Wiggins?"

"Oh, rubbish!" His Lordship clenched his fists and took a deep breath. "Originally it wasn't you he was following, Hale. It was my daughter."

Hale was taken aback. "Your daughter?"

The peer nodded. "I knew she was up to something she didn't want me to know about, so of course I wanted to know what it was. Sarah has always been a bit wild, ever since her mother died."

"I'm completely lost," Hale said. "What does this have to do with me?"

"Hawkins followed her to that music hall several nights in a row. I couldn't imagine what she was doing there. Then she started to meet you late in the evening at the back entrance."

"But I don't even know your daughter!"

Sedgewood snorted. "Don't take me for a fool. Hawkins followed you all the way to some village on the Sussex Downs. Isn't that right, Hawkins? If you'd spent the night with her—" Apparently this horror was not to be contemplated, because Sedgewood didn't finish the sentence.

Hale, meanwhile, was lost in a horror of his own as the truth finally sunk in. Lord Sedgewood's daughter was his Sadie, and her real name was Sarah Bridgewater! He'd always suspected that "Sadie Briggs" was a stage name, perhaps borrowing the initials of Sarah Bernhardt. How wrong he'd been.

So this was why she had foiled every effort of his to find out about her background! What else had she lied to him about besides her name? In fact, had that feisty young lady told him the truth about anything?

"Seducing my daughter to get to me was beyond contempt, Mr. Hale," Sedgewood went on.

"I didn't seduce your daughter." *Not that I didn't want to.* "And I didn't know she was your daughter. I knew her as Sadie Briggs, a music hall singer."

Sedgewood sat down and with eyes that could kill turned to his man. "Hawkins? Is this true?" His voice trembled. "A music hall singer?"

Hawkins gripped his hat in his two hands. "I never followed her inside, Your Lordship. I didn't— That is, it never occurred to me to do so."

"You may go, Hawkins."

"Yes, sir. Thank you, sir."

Hawkins departed with the speed of a man who had just been granted a pardon.

Sedgewood, somehow looking smaller, regarded Hale and Gillette with a "what next?" expression.

"Come now, Your Lordship, certainly your daughter could have done far worse!" Gillette said.

"Yes, but she wouldn't have been doing it on stage. A music hall singer! This is intolerable. Thank God her dear mother is dead!" He put his head in his hands.

Sedgewood's late wife, Hale knew from his research, had been a minor royal. As an American, the whole nobility thing had never really resonated with Hale, much less the idea that performing on the stage was not respectable. But intellectually he understood that Sedgewood was feeling humiliated. Good!

Not taking time to sort out his own feelings about Sadie—Sarah! —he went on the attack.

"Were you being blackmailed by Madame Sosostris?" he asked Sedgewood.

Sedgewood looked up. "Certainly not! I've done nothing that I could be blackmailed about."

"Why did you visit her?"

"I was a fool to do that! It was all Balfour's fault. Somehow he mesmerized me into believing the silly woman could actually foretell the future. What balderdash! As soon as I heard that phony accent of hers I knew I'd made a mistake, but it was too late to back out. "

138

"Why was the future so important to you?" Gillette asked. "You give every indication of being deeply interested in the past—several thousand years in the past."

It didn't take a Sherlock Holmes to figure that out. Gillette was standing right next a black granite bust of the falcon-god Horus that would have looked right at home on the set of *The Ring of Thoth*. It was one of the Egyptian antiquities scattered around the library, like the statue of the cat-god Bastet that Hale had noticed on his first visit.

Sedgewood paced nervously. "I'd give a thousand pounds to know whether Howard Carter, Carnarvon's archeologist, is going to find anything significant in the Valley of the Kings. This competition between us has turned a bit ugly, as well as ruinously expensive. It's all over the trash papers. I'd just as soon call it quits, but I don't want to look like a fool."

"And what did Madame Sosostris tell you?" Hale said.

Sedgewood seemed not to notice that Hale's notebook was out. "She said that Carter would discover a major tomb, but not for several years. You know what I think? I think that somebody wants me to stay involved in Egypt, some enemy of mine who wants to see me waste a lot of time and money."

"I should think it far more likely, Your Lordship, that the clairvoyant was simply making a vague prediction that would scarcely be remembered by the time it will most likely be proved false," Gillette said. "It was probably her standard *modus operandi*."

"My question about blackmail, though perhaps offensive, wasn't frivolous," Hale said. "We have information that the woman did blackmail several of her clients, presumably men of very high station. If her death hadn't been part of a series, her victims would have been the first suspects."

Sedgewood stopped pacing. "I assure you again that I was not one of those victims. I only met the woman once."

"Did you know any of the other Hangman victims?" Hale asked.

"Who were they? I don't pay attention to all that sensationalism in the Press."

Hale, ignoring the slur on his work, named and described the other three victims.

"Such people were hardly likely to be part of my social circle," Sedgewood sniffed.

"Indeed," Gillette said with an air of finality. "Lord Sedgewood, I think it extremely unlikely that we or the police shall have to disturb you again."

"I am disturbed enough already, gentlemen. This news you have brought me about my daughter is . . ." Words failed him. "A music hall singer!"

"Times have changed, Your Lordship," Hale said. Perhaps Sedgewood, not the most progressive of men, didn't fully realize that the words "singer" or "actress" no longer meant "prostitute" or "courtesan."

"I am a peer of the realm, young man. My daughter does not sing in music halls. Nor does she consort with journalists."

Yes, she does, Eddie, old boy.

"No one knows that 'Sadie Briggs' is your daughter," Hale said. "She didn't even tell me. Not that it's any of your business, but our relations haven't reached the conclusion you've jumped to, and I'm not sure they ever will. As her father, you might consider talking to her about all of this. I know I sure as hell plan to."

Hale was still hot long after he and Gillette had left Lord Sedgewood's townhouse. They walked for blocks in silence, each thinking his own thoughts.

"If I weren't so mad at Sadie, I'd apologize to her," Hale said. "She was right about the bearded man following us at the train station."

"Well, it's nice to have one mystery solved," Gillette said, "but there's still the small matter of the other bearded man—the one who killed O'Quinn and probably the other three as well."

TWENTY-THREE
Sadie Sings

"I am accustomed to have mystery at one end of my
cases, but to have it at both ends is too confusing."
   – Sherlock Holmes, "The Adventure of the
   Illustrious Client"

Hale went to the Alhambra that night for the debut
performance of a new solo artist. Sadie—he would always
think of her that way—sang so beautifully that he almost
cried.

Unable to wait a moment longer than necessary, he
met her just outside her dressing room door instead of at
their usual place at the back of the music hall on Charing
Cross Road.

"Enoch!" She hugged him.

"You were wonderful, Sarah."

"Do you really think—uh-oh." The look on her face
reminded Hale of her father, a resemblance he found
surprisingly painful. "You know."

"So does your father. We had a long talk this
afternoon."

She slumped against the wall. "I'm doomed."

"You were right about the man with the beard at Charing Cross Station. He was a fellow named Hawkins who your father hired to follow you. He wasn't very good at it, and Gillette spotted him." Hale had told her about Gillette the night before. "With some persuasion, he identified Lord Sedgewood as his employer. So that makes you, who—Lady Sarah, I suppose?"

She stuck out her chin, which Hale found quite attractive. "I am Sadie Briggs and I am a wonderful singer. You said so yourself, Enoch Hale."

"You're also a wonderful liar. Why did you really stop seeing me? Why did you start again? What do you know about the murders that you haven't told me?"

"I never lied to you, except for using my stage name. I just avoided telling you certain things. And I don't know anything but what I told you about Mr. Powers, which is almost nothing! I stopped seeing you because you said you were going to talk to my father and I was afraid of what you were going to find out. But I missed you too much, that's why I came back to you. How could you think there was anything else, you infuriating man!"

"Maybe because you've been deceiving me since the evening we met."

"You mean in not telling you my life story? Oh, Enoch, don't you see? When you told me all about your family and how you didn't want to be what they wanted you to be, I knew that you were just like me. But I also knew you wouldn't be interested in Lady Sarah."

"You could have let me decide that for myself, you know."

"And what would you have decided?"

By way of answer, Hale grabbed her and kissed her. At first she seemed startled, but apparently she got used to it. The embrace went on for quite a while. The sound of clapping from three wise-guy stagehands made him break it off. He didn't appreciate having an audience.

"I guess I made a mistake," Sadie said breathlessly. She pulled him into her dressing room. Hale looked around. It was small.

"You know this will cause talk, the two of us alone in here."

Sadie wrapped her arms around him.

"Say, you should have seen William Gillette with your father," Hale said. "He's been playing Sherlock Holmes so long he acts just like him. He even had that guy Hawkins convinced that he *was* Holmes. I bet he could have fooled Wiggins . . ."

He stopped, struck by an idea.

"Do you really want to talk about that now?" Sadie murmured into his ear.

There was a knock on the door. Hale wasn't as disturbed by the interruption as he normally would have been in such a situation. He wanted to think about something.

"Go away," Sadie yelled.

The knocking continued, harder.

Sadie sighed, clearly exasperated. "Why now?" she muttered as she disengaged from Hale. She opened the door of the dressing room.

Edward Bridgewater, the Earl of Sedgewood, stood in the hallway, looking like a fish out of water. "Sarah—"

"Hello, Father," she said coolly. She wiped her hands on her silk dress. "I'm called Sadie here."

Lord Sedgewood swallowed hard. "Can we talk . . . Sadie?"

Sadie looked at Hale. "I was just leaving," he said.

"Wait for me," she said. "The usual place in fifteen minutes."

"Make it half an hour," he said. "I have something to do first. And you two might need the time, too."

TWENTY-FOUR
Mr. Sherlock Holmes

It is not enough to say that William Gillette resembles Sherlock Holmes. Sherlock Holmes looks exactly like William Gillette.
    – Orson Welles

After a visit to Scotland Yard, where Hale found Chief Inspector Wiggins still doggedly at his desk as expected, Hale was fifteen minutes late for the rendezvous with Sadie. But Sadie was even later. She came out of the Alhambra with her father about ten minutes after Hale's return and a moment before he would have decided that she must have left without him.

Displaying all the emotion of a plaster bust, Lord Sedgewood kissed his daughter on the cheek and nodded at Hale before walking brusquely down Leicester Square.

"How did it go?" Hale asked, taking Sadie's arm.

"Better than I expected. He didn't shout. And he actually listened to me. Fancy that!"

146

"So he's reconciled to having a daughter who's a music hall singer madly infatuated with a Fleet Street journalist?"

"Oh, no! I think he's simply decided that Lady Sarah and Sadie Briggs are two different people who just happen to inhabit the same body. And he's right, actually." She squeezed Hale's arm. "You will continue to call me Sadie, won't you?"

"I couldn't do otherwise."

"Oh, and Father still hates the Press. Who said I was infatuated?"

"You implied it. Remind me to hate your father."

"One can't hate him, really. He's just an old-fashioned stick in the mud. The legitimate theater has been respectable since Sir Henry Irving. Music hall is just a little behind on that."

"Well," said Hale, "I certainly hope journalism never becomes respectable. That would take all the fun out of it."

Tom Eliot was waiting for them, as usual, at Murray's Night Club. Sherlock Holmes surely would have counted the cigarette stubs to figure out how much the banker poet had been smoking, Hale mused. And then he'd probably have deduced the number of martinis consumed from the glaze in Eliot's eye.

"Ah, the lovely Sadie and what's his name." Eliot closed the book he was reading, *Trent's Last Case*. "How goes the sleuthing, Enoch?"

"It's been an interesting day." After placing a drink order with a bouncy waitress, Hale described his morning encounter with John Hawkins.

"And why would this Lord Sedgewood want to have you followed in the first place?" Eliot demanded.

How could Hale answer that without revealing Sadie's true identity? He didn't see a way short of outright lying, and that made life much too complicated. Hale sent Sadie a look imbedded with a silent question. She smiled across the table and nodded slightly, giving her approval to tell the whole story.

But before Hale could do that, Chief Inspector Henry Wiggins entered the nightclub in the company of a by-now familiar figure, his height and hawkish nose distinctive way across the room. Hale waved at them.

"We're getting company," he told his table mates. "I asked them to join us."

Instinctively, the two men at the table stood up.

"Tom, I want you to meet Chief Inspector Wiggins," Hale said. "And I understand you've met the other gentleman."

Eliot put out his hand. "Yes, it's a pleasure to see you again, Mr. Holmes."

"Holmes!" Sadie exclaimed. "Are you *Sherlock* Holmes?"

"I suppose if I denied it you wouldn't believe me." Holmes spoke in his normal voice, the American accent discarded like a false mustache.

"Very cute," Hale said. "When we confronted Hawkins, you had me convinced that you were Gillette pretending to be Holmes. I thought you were fooling Hawkins, but you were really fooling me."

Sadie looked from Holmes to Hale. "You've lost me good and proper. I don't understand, Enoch."

"I only figured it out a couple of hours ago. When I told you Gillette was so much like Sherlock Holmes that he could have fooled Wiggins, who'd known the real Holmes years ago, suddenly it clicked. Back at the Islington Studios the man I knew as Gillette called Wiggins 'Chief Inspector.' But Wiggins had never used his title and neither had I. So how did he know that Wiggins was a chief inspector? Because he knew Wiggins.

"In fact, when we first came across Holmes in the studio Wiggins was just about to call out his name."

148

"That's true," Wiggins inserted.

"But Holmes announced himself as Gillette to keep him from doing that. Then later, when he had a chance to interview Ruby Alexander, he avoided her. I thought he was just being coy because of some past attachment or conflict, but it was because Miss Alexander would have known the real Gillette from working with him on the stage. He could fool everyone else because he looked like Gillette to those who'd only seen him on film. His voice was no giveaway because moviegoers have never heard it. All he had to do was adopt an American accent, which I seem to recall he once did for a two-year stretch."

"That is quite sound," said Sherlock Holmes, "and even accurate."

"Another clue, which I missed at the time, was the ease with which Gillette restrained Hawkins, displaying both strength and a fighting skill for which actors are not especially known. Sherlock Holmes, on the other hand, once twisted a bent poker back into shape with his bare hands."

"I really must congratulate you, Mr. Hale," Holmes said. "You have done quite well indeed."

"Well, I would have known who you were from the beginning," Eliot told Holmes, "because we met at Lloyd's. Why the masquerade?"

"It is an essential skill of the consulting detective to be able to adapt to circumstances and to seize opportunities," Holmes said, sliding into a seat. The others sat down as well. "When the guard at Islington Studios recognized me as Gillette, I accepted the identification without hesitation. When I was still in regular practice as a detective, my absence from London tended to excite the criminal classes. Now that I am retired, my presence tends to do the same. I find that even after all these years away from the playing field my reputation remains rather inflated, thanks to friend Watson's romanticized accounts of our cases. I can move about with considerably more freedom if I adopt a *nom de guerre* or disguise."

"How were you disguised when you killed Powers?" Hale demanded. "Or Sosostris? Or Alcock?"

"Enoch!" Sadie cried.

Holmes raised his eyebrows. "You're full of surprises, Mr. Hale."

Eliot looked at Hale as if he was a madman, and Hale wasn't sure he was wrong. But he'd gone this far. He had to press on, sounding more confident than he felt.

"I have to admit that I didn't figure it out by myself," he said. "Horace Harker gave me the idea."

"He's still alive?" Holmes murmured. "Surely he can't still be working for Central News Syndicated!"

"Not really, but he hasn't quite figured that out yet. Harker realized that you are just the sort of person to take the law into your own hands to punish these criminals that the official police couldn't touch."

"But O'Quinn wasn't a criminal," Holmes protested. "That was an essential clue that helped me deduce who did kill all four of the Hangman victims."

"What he says is true," said Wiggins, who had been an interested but mostly silent observer until now. "We've heard back from the American police and they don't know of any rumors or suspicions involving him in the States."

Hale felt as though he were sinking. "Then what were you doing at Islington if not to kill O'Quinn?" he asked Holmes.

"I followed you there."

"But I didn't see— Oh, never mind. Let's hear it from the beginning."

Before he could begin, the waitress brought their drinks. Hale took a healthy gulp of his Manhattan.

"The beginning," said Holmes, "was when I first read about these Hangman murders in my local newspaper.

Although I have been retired for some time, I have not ceased to be interested in the criminal world that was my bread and cheese for almost thirty years. I began to form a few preliminary theories about the business, but I had to come to London to check them out."

"Is that where you were when we came knocking on your cottage door?" Sadie asked, gin fizz in hand.

Holmes nodded. "Indeed. That very day I received a full report of your visit from Harold Sackhurst. I should say his description of you two was accurate in every regard." Holmes's gray eyes lingered on Sadie's fair features longer than Hale would have expected from the few Holmes adventures he had read. He doubted that the detective was the misogynist that came across in Watson's writings.

"Your name was already familiar to me, Mr. Hale, from reading your newspaper stories," Holmes went on. "In fact, I had begun to suspect you."

"Me!" What was this, a counter-attack? "That's nonsense!"

"Not at all. Your stories contained a level of detail seldom found in the Press dispatches. Now I realize that detail came from an excellent eye for observation combined with inside information provided to you exclusively by Chief Inspector Wiggins." He shook his head mockingly. "That just isn't done, Wiggins."

The Scotland Yard official smiled. "Right you are, sir. It's quite irregular."

Holmes and Wiggins seem to be having a fine old time. Hale's stomach was beginning to sour.

"So I began to follow you, Mr. Hale, to see what you were up to." Holmes contorted his face, instantly looking like an old man. "Flowers for your girl, sir?" he said in a creaky Cockney voice. "Yes, I observed your exchange with Commander Bond outside the Alhambra that night in the guise of an old flower seller. And I followed you the next day to the Islington Studios."

Floundering, trying to rescue some shred of dignity from the situation, Hale said, "This is all very interesting, but following me didn't do anything to solve the four murders."

Holmes set down his whiskey, a look of surprise on his face. "On the contrary, Mr. Hale, I'm quite confident that I know who the murderer is. Unfortunately, proving it is an entirely different matter."

TWENTY-FIVE
The Final Unmasking

> "It is not what we know but what we can prove."
> – Sherlock Holmes, *The Hound of the Baskervilles*

"You can leave proving it to the Yard, Mr. Holmes," Wiggins said.

The detective shook his head. "I'm afraid not, Wiggins. There is a way to deal with this, but it will have to be outside of officials channels."

Wiggins studied his coffee. "I didn't hear that."

"None of us did," Eliot volunteered, and quickly turned the conversation to a question that had always bothered him about the adventure of the Red-Headed League. ("Where did they go with all the dirt?") Hale was too keyed up wondering what was next to pay any attention.

After another hour of conversation and booze, Eliot and Wiggins left. Holmes looked across the table at Hale. "I need your help."

"I'd be glad to give it, especially if there's a story in it for me."

Holmes shook his head. "Not soon. Perhaps some day, when it can no longer do any harm, I will give you permission to publish a record of these events with all the names and even the year disguised as the faithful Watson has done so often."

"Why me?" Hale asked.

"That will become clear when I tell you what I want you to do. For now, though, this will have to remain between us. I mean, just us." He looked pointedly at Sadie.

She stood up. "I don't need a pyramid to fall on me. I can take a hint."

"Sadie—" Hale began.

"Oh, it's all right, love. I don't care about your boring old mystery anyway. I'll see you tomorrow. Sweet dreams."

Not much chance of that, Hale thought. He had a bad feeling about this. He was afraid to go along with Holmes, but more afraid not to.

He gave Sadie a quick kiss. She flounced off, shooting daggers at Holmes on the way.

"Okay," Hale said. "What's the deal?"

"I need you to send Commander Ian Bond a telegram and ask him to meet you tomorrow at noon in your flat. Tell him that you have vital information for him about the Irish Republican Army."

"But he won't give me the time of day!"

"I believe that he will respond to that particular message."

Hale didn't know which question to ask first because he had so many. He settled on, "Why a telegram? I could just call him on the telephone."

"On the telephone, he would ask you a dozen questions that we don't want to answer. He won't take the time to send you a return telegram to do that."

"How does Bond fit in?"

"At this point I can only assure you that he's absolutely key to unmasking the murderer."

154

"What do you know about Bond, other than seeing him talk to me outside the Alhambra?"

"I know that he works for my brother."

The penny dropped, and Holmes must have seen it on Hale's face. "In Watson's roman à clef about what he called the Bruce-Partington plans," Holmes said, "he quoted me as saying that Mycroft occasionally *is* the British government. That was as close as Watson dare come to the truth that my brother works in the shadows as director of His Majesty's Secret Service. Even at Whitehall his name is usually not mentioned."

"Just an initial," Hale muttered.

"Precisely so. I believe that is all you need to know at the moment."

"Not quite. Where do I find Bond?"

"Here's the cable address." Holmes scribbled on a sheet of paper in his notebook. He tore it off and gave it to Hale.

"Did you forget anything else?"

"Do you own a gun, Hale?"

"No, I haven't found journalism that dangerous. At least, not until now."

"Well, don't worry about it."

Yeah, right, Hale thought. Don't worry about it.

Bond showed up five minutes early at Hale's flat on Claverton Street near St. George Square. Fortunately, Holmes had arrived ten minutes before that. At the knock on the door, the detective disappeared into Hale's bedroom.

"Come in, Commander."

"What's this all about?" Bond said without preamble as he stepped into the flat. "If you lured me here on a pretext to try to get an interview out of me, I warn you that it won't work."

Holmes stepped into the room, nonchalantly facing Bond with his hands in his pocket. "It's a little more serious than that, Commander Bond."

"Who the hell are you?" Bond's Scottish burr became more pronounced, presumably under the stress of the situation.

"I am Sherlock Holmes. More importantly, Commander, you are the man who has been somewhat fancifully dubbed the Hangman Killer."

Bond's hand quickly moved to his breast pocket. Just as quickly, Sherlock Holmes pulled out a revolver and aimed it squarely at the naval officer. "Both this Webley and its owner have been around a long time, Commander, but I assure you that they are still in working order."

Bond slowly withdrew his hand to show that it contained a cigar case. "What the hell are you talking about?"

Good question, Hale thought. His brain hadn't had time to process what his eyes and ears had taken in.

"It was not, I regret to say, perfectly obvious from the first," Holmes said. "I was initially sidetracked by the most obvious commonality among the first three victims. They were all criminals. Powers and Fogarty, to use her real name, had been behind bars in the past and were still active, although unproven, villains. Alcock was believed to be a forger and counterfeiter, although that too was unproven. But Rory O'Quinn broke that mold. Scotland Yard's inquiries and my own using somewhat less respectable sources confirmed that he wasn't involved in anything so venal as crime for profit.

"What, then, did all four victims have in common that might cause someone to kill them—and in particular to kill them in a way that strongly suggested execution, the same fate that met Sir Roger Casement and so many others?"

"They were all Irish," Hale said. The reference to Casement had suddenly made it clear to Hale. Casement was the former British diplomat hanged for treason just after the Easter Rising of '16, to the chagrin of Doyle, Yeats and Shaw, and the gratification of Churchill and Balfour.

Holmes nodded, not for a moment taking his eyes off of Bond, who was coolly putting a cigar into his mouth.

"Our friends in the Irish Republican Army have been quite busy of late, stealing explosives for use in Ireland and burning farms outside of London in retaliation for the burnings by Mr. Churchill's Black and Tans in Ireland. Fifty members of the Parliament and Cabinet have been under special protection since last year because of IRA threats against their lives.

"I've often noted that a clue which seems to point one way can mean something very different when approached from another direction. Burglary, blackmail, and forgery are all skills that can be used not only in private crime, but also in furtherance of espionage and insurgency. I began to suspect that all three of the Hangman's victims were involved with the IRA or some other violent group seeking Irish independence."

"So that's why Alcock had the makings of incendiary devices in his shop," Hale said.

"Exactly," the detective agreed. "Hence brother Mycroft's concern about the excessive energies of an ambitious Press reporter who might upset the apple cart. He undoubtedly had his own plan for protecting the Empire's interests, and exposure in the Press was not part of it."

Hale had a question about Fogarty/Sosostris and the Minister of War and Air, but he didn't get to ask it then.

Bond returned the cigar case to his breast pocket. "But how do you figure that O'Quinn fit in? You said yourself that he wasn't bent." Bond sounded curious but not concerned. Looking at his muscled body and casual manner, Hale suspected that the handsome Scot was possibly the most dangerous man he had ever encountered.

"O'Quinn had a growing fame, a substantial income, and the ability to travel around the world without suspicion," Holmes said. "All of those are of considerable value to the Irish rebels. O'Quinn was an Irish-American, of course, and I can assure you upon my word as Altamont that there is no Irishman quite as Irish as an American one. The New York Police, after some further inquiries in the right places, have confirmed to Scotland Yard that O'Quinn was a member of Clan-na-Gael. That's an American secret society that provides funds to their friends in Ireland.

"Powers, Fogarty, Alcock, and O'Quinn were all members of a conspiracy of Irish rebels, perhaps known to each other, perhaps not. They must have all been involved in a particular plot that Commander Bond, acting independently of His Majesty's Secret Service, decided to foil in the simplest way possible—by killing all of them in a way that would scare off any other conspirators. I believe that Daniel Day, the tobacconist, must have been one of them who took the hint and disappeared. He hasn't been seen since the day of his neighbor's murder. I suspect that he's alive and well in Ireland."

Bond waved his unlit cigar. "That all sounds plausible enough, except for the part about me. I don't have any interest in the IRA."

"Oh, come, Commander Bond! Your actions belie that claim. You repeatedly refused to speak with Hale in any meaningful way, and yet you agreed to meet with him here at his flat when he dangled the promise of information about the IRA.

"As for your involvement in the murders, that part really is elementary. My examination of the scene at Islington Studios traced the footprints from the fire escape to the point where you murdered O'Quinn. They belonged to a man approximately six-foot-one and wearing square-toed boots—those very boots, Commander." Holmes pointed and Bond looked down.

Hale tensed, feeling that if Bond were going to make a move it would come soon.

"Ezra Pound almost caught you after the act. You were just leaving after having hanged Alcock when he arrived. With admirable presence of mind, however, you simply pretended to be arriving instead of leaving. As Scotland Yard's investigation into Powers's murder continued and Hale poked around in this business uncowed, you got nervous and went back to the Alhambra to make sure you hadn't left any clues behind. Hale saw you there and assumed you were trying to uncover the killer, but just the opposite was true. Having been spotted twice, you prudently donned a false beard when you went to the Islington Studios the next day to kill Rory O'Quinn.

"Have I left anything out?"

"Yes," Bond said. "Any shred of proof."

"Oh, I can't prove that you are the Hangman," Holmes said. Hale thought his grip on the revolver seemed to tighten. "But I don't need to. The purpose of this gun is not to march you down to Scotland Yard. I have a much harsher fate in mind for you. You see, Commander, I still have contacts among the Irish from some previous adventures. My plan is simply to enlighten them as to who killed their comrades. I am fairly sure that will be the end of the Hangman."

For the first time Bond seemed to lose his composure. "You fool! You traitor! You have no idea what you're getting involved with. Those pigs were small cogs in a big wheel—a plot to assassinate the Prime Minister in retaliation for the death of Terence MacSwiney during his hunger strike. They were bound for the gallows anyway. I was just hurrying the process."

"We are a nation of laws and justice," Holmes said calmly. "We cannot have the latter without the former."

"You're a fine one to talk! You played judge, jury, and sometimes executioner your entire career."

"Perhaps with age comes wisdom."

Bond lit his cigar. "I don't think so, Mr. Bloody Righteous Holmes." He flicked the cigar at Holmes. Almost as the projectile flew out of his fingers it exploded in a riot of noise and smoke. Hale bent over, coughing and flailing his arms in a futile attempt to clear the clouds. He heard a door slam shut and boots click on the stairs.

He made his way to a window, opened it, and hung out, gasping for breath.

When the smoke finally cleared, Sherlock Holmes was sitting in one of Hale's chairs with a mildly nettled look on his face.

"What the hell was that?" Hale asked.

"Offhand, I should say it was a defensive weapon provided by my brother to his agents. He has a man who spends his time dreaming up such things."

TWENTY-SIX
The End of the Hangman

Human kind
Cannot bear very much reality.
— T.S. Eliot, "Burnt Norton"

"This place will never be the same," Hale muttered.

"Apparently Commander Bond has a penchant for dramatic exits," Holmes commented. "I suppose one should have expected that from a man who uses a hangman's rope as a murder weapon, although I daresay he would consider it an instrument of justice. At any rate, he could have just walked away without all the smoke."

"Speaking of just walking away, why didn't the plotters kill Churchill while he was in their hands at Madame Sosostris's place?" This was the question Hale hadn't had the chance to ask before. "I thought of that as soon as I knew they were Irish rebels. And if they were avenging the work of the Black and Tans, it would only make sense for them to kill the man who created the unit, either in addition to or instead of Lloyd George."

"Churchill only visited Air Street once, with a bodyguard from Scotland Yard, and probably didn't announce himself in advance."

161

Hale remembered the humorless bodyguard.

"They had no chance to blackmail him for the same reasons," Holmes went on, "but I'm sure that all of the other clients of Madame Sosostris in sensitive positions have been scrutinized by His Majesty's Secret Service to make sure they haven't been blackmailed into betraying King and Country."

Hale couldn't imagine Churchill being susceptible to blackmail anyway. Every newly exposed foible of his—and there were many—seemed to delight his indulgent admirers and make no difference to his foes.

"At least we've seen the end of the Hangman," Hale said.

In that, he was wrong.

Three days later, he met Sadie for lunch at Simpson's. *The Daily Telegraph*, sitting on their table when she arrived, carried the headline **HANGMAN STRIKES AGAIN** over a Central Press Syndicate story by Enoch Hale.

"I just don't understand," Sadie said. She picked up the story and read:

> The body of Commander Ian Bond, 32, of the Royal Navy, was found hanged Wednesday in his flat in the Serpentine Mews.
>
> "All indications are this is the work of the Hangman," said Chief Inspector Henry Wiggins of the Metropolitan Police Service.
>
> Commander Bond, late of His Majesty's Royal Navy, had a distinguished career in the Great War. He entered the Navy in 1908, and was three times mentioned in dispatches and awarded the DSO.

Born in Glencoe, Scotland, on July 14, 1888, he was the younger of two brothers. He is survived by his older brother, Andrew, his brother's wife, Monique, and a nephew . . .

"But that's not true!" Sadie said, looking up from the newspaper. "You know he wasn't killed by the Hangman."

Unable to repress his reporter's instincts completely, Hale had told Sadie the whole story two days ago and made her promise on her mother's grave not to tell another living soul.

"It's true that Wiggins said it," Hale retorted. "Who am I, a humble journalist and a Yankee, to correct a chief inspector of Scotland Yard?"

"The Irish rebels got him."

"Maybe, maybe not," Hale said. "He could have hanged himself because he didn't see any other way out. Or M could have saved him the trouble."

"I'll try not to believe that." Sadie went back to *The Daily Telegraph*. As her eyes moved across the page to the photo of Ian Bond staring out at her, she cried out. "Enoch, I've seen that man!"

"Where?"

"I'm not sure. But somehow I have a feeling it was at the Alhambra."

"Recently?"

"Maybe in the last few weeks."

A chill crept along Hale's spine. "You must have seen him the evening he killed Powers. But he must have not seen you, luckily. If he'd viewed you as a threat, you can be certain you wouldn't be sitting here."

Sadie shivered and took a long drink of wine. "I still find the whole thing shocking. Military men are so disciplined, aren't they? Following orders is their whole life.

It's so hard to believe that he would just go off on his own and start killing people as a free agent."

Hale set down his own glass. "It is, isn't it?"

TWENTY-SEVEN
After the End

"Well, well, I suppose I shall have to compound a felony as usual."

– Sherlock Holmes, "The Adventure of the Three Gables"

Enoch Hale went down to Sussex on Saturday, this time by himself. As he looked at the hills gently rolling down to the sea, he found it hard to credit Sherlock Holmes's comment about crime in the country. Watson had quoted it in one of the *Adventures*, the one about Copper Beeches. How did it go? Oh, yes. "The lowest and vilest alleys in London do not present a more dreadful record of sin than does the smiling and beautiful countryside."

If that were true, Hale certainly saw no evidence of it as he knocked on the door of Holmes's villa. An old woman answered, well padded and slightly bent, but with a kind face balanced by shrewd eyes.

"Yes?"

"I'm here to see Mr. Holmes."

"Is he expecting you, sir?"

Hale had not called ahead. "I rather think that he is, although perhaps not this soon."

Within a few moments Holmes appeared. Even in this bucolic surrounding he radiated contained energy, like a coil ready to spring.

"Are you he here to see my bees, Mr. Hale? They really are remarkable creatures. There are no rogue bees, you know, or at least no criminals. But, then, one could argue that there are no individual bees, either. For them it's all about the hive. I wonder whether the trade-off is worth it."

Hale hadn't called on Holmes to discuss philosophy. "Bond wasn't a rogue, was he?"

Holmes pierced the reporter with his gray eyes. "Full marks for getting right to the point, Hale. But what makes you say that?"

"It came to me as I was talking to Sadie. A man like Bond wouldn't act alone. That would be against all his training as a military man. No, he was just the instrument in a Secret Service plan to stop the rebel plot in a way that didn't panic the British public about the Irish, but at the same time sent a message to the conspirators."

"For God's sake, man, you didn't tell Miss Briggs, did you?"

"No. I kept the notion to myself until now because I wasn't sure. Now I am, thanks to you."

Holmes sat down. Hale faced him in the chair opposite.

"I was hoping you wouldn't find out, Hale. This is dangerous knowledge."

"Who's behind it? Is this an independent project of His Majesty's Secret Service or does the Government know?"

"Let's just say that His Majesty Himself is aware that certain agents of His Government are operating with a virtual license to kill."

Hale snorted. "I'm sure that sounds impressive when they're talking to recruits, but staffing must be difficult given the life expectancy on the job. So who got Bond—the Irish, the British, or himself?"

Holmes lit a long pipe. "Believe me, Mr. Hale, this is something you don't want to know."

All of a sudden, Hale got it. He had the final piece. "Bond isn't dead, is he?"

"Didn't you see the body? My old friend Wiggins usually calls you to the scene."

"I saw a body, but the face was already covered. That didn't happen all the other times."

The old detective sighed. "Since you already know too much for your own good, young man, you might as well know the rest. The body was that of a criminal duly sentenced by a jury of his peers and legally executed under the law of England."

"And what about Bond?"

"He doesn't have friends or a close family. That's why he was chosen for the assignment. He will continue serving the Crown in another place under another name."

"I suppose M told you all of this?"

"Not a word. What I have shared with you are my deductions. I have not the slightest doubt, however, that they are correct in every particular."

Hale stood up, furious. He'd been wrong about one thing; there *was* evil in the countryside. "This doesn't even bother you, does it?"

"I've lived a long time, Hale. My brother has lived even longer. One of the things we have both learned is that emotions are a luxury at best and harmful at worst. You really would do well to swallow your indignation and try to forget what you guessed and I deduced. The knowledge that you have is not safe for you. Believe me, I know M."

Hale started to open the door, planning to leave without another word. But he stopped and looked back. "Watson was wrong."

The figure in the chair raised his eyebrows quizzically.

"This executioner was no amateur," Hale said.

He slammed the door behind him on his way out.

About the Authors

Dan Andriacco has been reading mysteries since he discovered Sherlock Holmes at the age of nine, and writing them almost as long. The first three books in his popular Sebastian McCabe – Jeff Cody series are *No Police Like Holmes*, *Holmes Sweet Holmes*, and *The 1895 Murder*. Coming soon is *The Disappearance of Mr. James Phillimore*.

A member of the Tankerville Club, a scion society of The Baker Street Irregulars, since 1981, he is also the author of *Baker Street Beat: An Eclectic Collection of Sherlockian Scribblings*. Follow his blog at www.danandriacco.com, his tweets at @*DanAndriacco*, and his Facebook Fan Page at www.facebook.com/DanAndriaccoMysteries.

Dr. Dan and his wife, Ann, have three grown children and five grandchildren. They live in Cincinnati, Ohio, USA.

Kieran McMullen discovered Holmes and Watson at an early age. His father, a university English professor, found his reading skills lacking and so, the summer of his eighth year assigned him the task of reading the complete Doyle stories before school started again in September.

After a twenty-two-year career in the US Army, twelve years in law enforcement and twenty years as a volunteer fireman, Kieran turned to writing about his favorite literary characters, Holmes and Watson. His first book, *Watson's Afghan Adventure*, centers on Watson's war experience before he met Holmes. His subsequent novels, *Sherlock Holmes and the Mystery of the Boer Wagon* and *Sherlock Holmes and the Irish Rebels*, concentrate on the duo's wartime experiences.

Kieran and his wife, Helen, live north of Darien, Georgia, on a few acres with their Irish Wolfhounds and Percheron draft horses. They have three children and six grandchildren.

Notes for the Curious

Some of the characters portrayed here have been historical, while the others existed only in the imaginations of the writers. For those that are curious, we present a few facts on the real life people who were involved.

Sarah Bernhardt: Probably one of the best-known names in the history of the theater, Sarah was born 22 October 1844, the child of a Dutch courtesan. Her father is unknown. At the age of 16 she became an actress. Her name became synonymous with dramatic presentation. By the time of our adventure she was well on in years but still acting. She was one of the earliest actors in motion pictures, starting in 1900. In fact, she might be credited with being in the first talking picture, *Le Duel d'Hamlet.* An Edison cylinder recording was played along with the film. If properly synchronized, it made the characters appear to talk. She was a great French patriot, a friend of Houdini, and a greatly loved performer.

Winston Churchill: Almost all modern readers are familiar with Winston Churchill as the Prime Minister who led the British Empire to victory in World War II. Many may not be as aware of his role in the Boer War, the disaster that was Gallipoli in the Great War, the establishment of the Black and Tans (a supplementary force to the Royal Irish Constabulary with one of the most horrific records of state-sponsored terrorism), or his plans to invade Ireland during World War II. He was a natural target for Irish War of Independence forces.

Lord Arthur Balfour: Born in 1848 and living until 1930, Lord Balfour was Prime Minister from 1902 until 1905. A close friend of Winston Churchill, he was Chief Secretary of Ireland from 1887 to 1891 during the "Irish Land Wars." Balfour ruled with an iron fist under the "Perpetual Crimes Act," which was aimed at preventing

170

boycotts, intimidation, and assembly. His nickname in Ireland, among the Nationalists, was Bloody Balfour. He became First Lord of the Admiralty after Churchill's Gallipoli disaster cost him the post. In 1916, Balfour became Foreign Secretary.

William Butler Yeats: At the time of our adventure Yeats was about 55 years of age. He was born to an Anglo-Irish family. His father was an artist and his mother an avid storyteller of Irish tales and legends. Yeats was deeply involved in Theosophy, Hermeticism, and Hinduism. He hated Catholicism and considered priests as controllers and manipulators. He was in love for years with Maude Gonne, an ardent Irish nationalist, but his love was not returned. He was good friends with Ezra Pound and a supporter of Mussolini and fascism.

Ezra Pound: Born in 1885 in Hailey, Idaho Territory, he was an only child. He worked as an editor in England in the early part of the twentieth century. His poetry was part of the early modernist movement. Because of his position he was able to promote the works of such people as T.S. Eliot, Robert Frost, James Joyce, and Ernest Hemingway. He did not see fit to fight in the Great War and blamed capitalism for the war. Pound became a great supporter of Mussolini and Hitler. He made hundreds of anti-US radio broadcasts during World War II. As a result he was tried for treason and spent a number of months incarcerated in Italy. He was determined to be unfit to stand trial and was sent to a mental ward for twelve years. He was finally released in 1958 and returned to Italy, where he died in 1972.

T.S. Eliot: Thomas Stearns Eliot was born in 1888 in St. Louis, Missouri. He would become a publisher, playwright, social and literary critic. In 1914, he immigrated to England and became a British citizen in 1927. He became friends with Ezra Pound, who was instrumental in having Eliot's classic poem, "The Love Song of J. Alfred Prufrock," published in 1915. He was one of the great poets of the twentieth century. He was awarded the Nobel Prize in Literature in 1948. But like most artists, his art did not bring wealth as well as fame, so he worked as a schoolteacher, a banker, and an editor. He died in London in 1965.

George Bernard Shaw: Shaw was also a winner of the Nobel Prize in Literature, his coming in 1925. Shaw was born in Dublin, Ireland, in 1856. This Irish dramatist would write sixty plays over his career, many of them a kind of black comedy. In 1938, he won an Oscar for his adaptation of *Pygmalion* to the big screen. Shaw spent much of his life involved in social problems and was a great advocate of equal rights, and communal ownership of productive farmlands, and mining. Shaw died in 1950.

Alfred Joseph Hitchcock: Hitch was born in London in 1899 and died in Bel Air, California, in 1980. When Mr. Hale met Hitch, the latter was working as an Inter-Title maker. That is, he penned the titles that led the viewer through the silent movie. He had a fairly difficult upbringing. His father was a strict disciplinarian and Hitch often felt wrongly accused. But the elder Hitchcock died when the son was just fourteen. Hitch left his Catholic school days behind to learn to be a draftsman. During the Great War he was considered too overweight to enlist, but by 1917 he had been accepted as a cadet in a local unit in London. He never saw action. His drafting background got him the job with Famous Players-Laskey Studios in Islington, which would become Gainsborough Pictures. Hitch went from writing titles to film director in five years. In time, of course, he came to be known as the "Master of Suspense." His early successes included such classics as *The Man Who Knew Too Much*, *The 39 Steps*, and *The Lady Vanishes*. In 1939 he moved to Hollywood where he became one of the most important directors of the twentieth century. He would also garner attention on radio and television.

Sherlock Holmes: It is generally agreed that he was born 6 January 1854. William S. Baring-Gould speculated that his education was rather broad in that his family frequently traveled the Continent and he was exposed to many customs and languages. Early in his formal education he found that he had an uncanny ability to use inductive and deductive reasoning to solve problems. He decided on a career as the world's first consulting detective. In January of 1881, Holmes was just beginning to make a name for himself. But it was his meeting with Dr. John H. Watson that month that would propel his career into the stuff of legends. In more than twenty years of active practice the team of Holmes and Watson changed the face of crime fighting. Holmes retired from the field at a still-young age and devoted himself to the keeping of bees and the occasional mystery that he could not resist. His obituary has never appeared in *The Times* of London.

Dan Andriacco and Kieran McMullen

A Word of Thanks

The authors would like to offer their special thanks for the support of the following people:

Ann Andriacco
Tony Andriacco
Steve Emecz
Helen McMullen
Jeff Suess

They also thank Arthur Conan Doyle for creating Sherlock Holmes, Dr. John H. Watson, Mycroft Holmes, Langdale Pike, and Shinwell Johnson.

Also from Kieran McMullen

  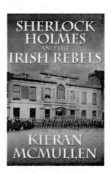

Three historical thrillers from the world's leading Sherlock Holmes military writer.

"Exciting, and full of authentic military detail"

The Sherlock Holmes Society of London.

Also from Dan Andriacco

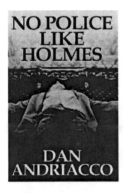 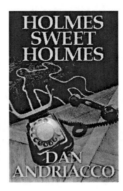 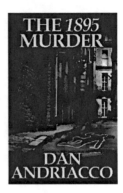

A series of modern murder-mysteries that all Sherlock Holmes fans will enjoy.

"No Police Like Holmes is an exciting and witty romp - not about Holmes but about his fans. The world's third-largest private collection of Sherlockiana has been donated to St Benignus, a small college in a small town in Ohio, and to celebrate, the college is hosting the Investigating Arthur Conan Doyle and Sherlock Holmes Colloquium. Jeff Cody, the college's PR director (and part-time crime writer), is an amused observer until the event is blighted by a real theft and a real murder, and he realises that there's rather a lot of suspects in deerstalkers. As if things weren't bad enough, Cody and his ex-girlfriend also become suspects."

The Sherlock Holmes Society of London

Also from Dan Andriacco groundbreaking
short story e-books

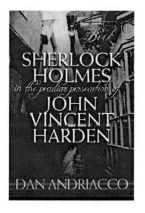 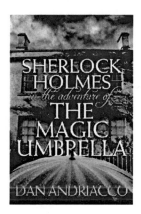

5 star reviews on Amazon Kindle

*"Dan Andriacco has written a great Sherlock Holmes short story; one
of the pastiches I've ever read."*

*"The plot is complex for such a short piece but remains very clean and
concise moving along rapidly to a surprising conclusion."*

CPSIA information can be obtained
at www.ICGtesting.com
Printed in the USA
LVOW10s2343210318
570756LV00007B/103/P